EX LIBRIS

_____
NAME

THE VILE VILLAGE

❋ A Series of Unfortunate Events ❋

THE BAD BEGINNING

THE REPTILE ROOM

THE WIDE WINDOW

THE MISERABLE MILL

THE AUSTERE ACADEMY

THE ERSATZ ELEVATOR

THE VILE VILLAGE

* A Series of Unfortunate Events *

BOOK *the Seventh*

THE VILE VILLAGE

by LEMONY SNICKET

Illustrations by Brett Helquist

WITHDRAWN

▬ HarperCollins*Publishers*

�֍

The Vile Village
Text copyright © 2001 by Lemony Snicket
Illustrations copyright © 2001 by Brett Helquist
A Series of Unfortunate Events Series Artwork © 2018 and Netflix, Inc.
All Rights Reserved.

Library of Congress Cataloging-in-Publication Data
Snicket, Lemony.
  The vile village / by Lemony Snicket ; illustrations by Brett Helquist.
    p. cm. — (A series of unfortunate events ; bk. 7)
  Summary: Under a new government program based on the saying "It takes a village to raise a child," the Baudelaire orphans are adopted by an entire town, with disastrous results.
  ISBN 978-0-06-440865-3 — ISBN 978-0-06-028890-7 (lib. bdg.)
ISBN 978-0-06-279617-2 (special edition)
  [1. Orphans—Fiction. 2. Brothers and sisters—Fiction. 3. City and town life—Fiction. 4. Humorous stories.] I. Helquist, Brett, ill. II. Title.
PZ7.S6795 Vi 2001   00-053511
[Fic]—dc21   CIP
                                                                    AC

18 19 20 21 22   PC/LSCH   80 79 78 77 76 75
❖
First Edition, 2001
Visit us on the World Wide Web! www.harpercollinschildrens.com

�֍

For Beatrice—
When we were together I felt breathless.
Now, you are.

THE VILE VILLAGE

No matter who you are, no matter where you live, and no matter how many people are chasing you, what you don't read is often as important as what you do read. For instance, if you are walking in the mountains, and you don't read the sign that says "Beware of Cliff" because you are busy reading a joke book instead, you may suddenly find yourself walking on air rather than on a sturdy bed of rocks. If you are baking a pie for your friends, and you read an article entitled "How to Build a Chair" instead of a cookbook, your pie will probably end up tasting like wood and nails instead of like crust and fruity filling. And if you insist on reading this book instead of something more cheerful, you will most certainly find yourself moaning in despair instead of wriggling in delight, so if you have any sense at all you will put this book down and pick up another one. I know of a book, for instance, called *The Littlest Elf,* which tells the story of a teensy-weensy little man who scurries around Fairyland having all sorts of adorable adventures, and you can see at once that you should probably read *The Littlest Elf* and wriggle over the lovely things that happened to this imaginary creature in a made-up place, instead of reading this book and moaning over the terrible things that happened to the three Baudelaire orphans in the village where I am now typing these very words. The misery, woe, and treachery contained in the pages of this book are so dreadful that it is important that you don't read any more of it than you already have.

The Baudelaire orphans, at the time this story begins, were certainly wishing that they weren't reading the newspaper that was in front of their eyes. A newspaper, as I'm sure you know, is a collection of supposedly true stories written down by writers who either saw them happen or talked to people who did. These writers are called journalists, and like telephone operators, butchers, ballerinas, and people who clean up after horses, journalists can sometimes make mistakes. This was certainly the case with the front page of the morning edition of *The Daily Punctilio*, which the Baudelaire children were reading in the office of Mr. Poe. "TWINS CAPTURED BY COUNT OMAR," the headline read, and the three siblings looked at one another in amazement over the mistakes that *The Daily Punctilio*'s journalists had made.

"'Duncan and Isadora Quagmire,'" Violet read out loud, "'twin children who are the only known surviving members of the Quagmire family, have been kidnapped by the notorious Count Omar. Omar is wanted by the police for a variety of dreadful crimes, and is easily recognized by his one long eyebrow, and the tattoo of an eye on his left ankle. Omar has also kidnapped Esmé Squalor, the city's sixth most important financial advisor, for reasons unknown.' Ugh!" The word "Ugh!" was not in the newspaper, of course, but was something Violet uttered herself as a way of saying she was too disgusted to read any further. "If I invented something as sloppily as this newspaper writes its stories," she said, "it would fall apart immediately." Violet, who at fourteen was the eldest Baudelaire child, was an excellent inventor, and spent a great deal of time with her hair tied up in a ribbon to keep it out of her eyes as she thought of new mechanical devices.

"And if I read books as sloppily," Klaus said, "I wouldn't remember one single fact." Klaus, the middle Baudelaire, had read more books than just about anyone his own age, which was almost thirteen. At many crucial moments, his sisters had relied on him to remember a helpful fact from a book he had read years before.

"Krechin!" Sunny said. Sunny, the youngest

Baudelaire, was a baby scarcely larger than a watermelon. Like many infants, Sunny often said words that were difficult to understand, like "Krechin!" which meant something along the lines of "And if I used my four big teeth to bite something as sloppily, I wouldn't even leave one toothmark!"

Violet moved the paper closer to one of the reading lamps Mr. Poe had in his office, and began to count the errors that had appeared in the few sentences she had read. "For one thing," she said, "the Quagmires aren't twins. They're triplets. The fact that their brother perished in the fire that killed their parents doesn't change their birth identity."

"Of course it doesn't," Klaus agreed. "And they were kidnapped by Count *Olaf*, not Omar. It's difficult enough that Olaf is always in disguise, but now the newspaper has disguised his name, too."

"Esmé!" Sunny added, and her siblings nodded. The youngest Baudelaire was talking about the part of the article that mentioned Esmé Squalor. Esmé and her husband, Jerome, had recently been the Baudelaires' guardians, and the children had seen with their own eyes that Esmé had not been kidnapped by Count Olaf. Esmé had secretly helped Olaf with his evil scheme, and had escaped with him at the last minute.

"And 'for reasons unknown' is the biggest mistake of all," Violet said glumly. "The reasons aren't unknown. *We* know them. We know the reasons Esmé, Count Olaf, and all of Olaf's associates have done so many terrible things. It's because they're terrible people." Violet put down *The Daily Punctilio*, looked around Mr. Poe's office, and joined her siblings in a sad, deep sigh. The Baudelaire orphans were sighing not only for the things they had read, but for the things they hadn't read. The article had not mentioned that both the Quagmires and the Baudelaires had lost their parents in terrible fires, and that both sets of parents had left enormous fortunes behind, and that Count Olaf had cooked up all of his evil plans just to get ahold of these fortunes for himself. The newspaper had failed to note that the Quagmire triplets had been kidnapped while trying to help the Baudelaires escape from Count Olaf's clutches, and that the Baudelaires had almost managed to rescue the Quagmires, only to find them snatched away once more. The journalists who wrote the story had not included the fact that Duncan Quagmire, who was a journalist himself, and Isadora Quagmire, who was a poet, each kept a notebook with them wherever they went, and that in their notebooks they had written down a terrible secret they had discovered about Count Olaf, but that all the Baudelaire orphans knew of this secret were the initials V.F.D., and that Violet, Klaus, and Sunny were always thinking of these three letters and what ghastly thing they could stand for. But most of all, the Baudelaire orphans had read no word about the fact that the Quagmire triplets were good friends of theirs, and that the three siblings were very worried about the Quagmires, and that every night when they tried to go to sleep, their heads were filled with terrible images of what could be happening to their friends, who were practically the only happy thing in the Baudelaires' lives since they received the news of the fire that killed their parents and began the series of unfortunate events that seemed to follow them wherever they went. The article in *The Daily Punctilio* probably did not mention these details because the journalist who wrote the story did not know about them, or did not think they were important, but the Baudelaires knew about them, and the three children sat together for a few moments and thought quietly about these very, very important details.

A fit of coughing, coming from the doorway of the office, brought them out of their thoughts, and the Baudelaires turned to see Mr. Poe coughing into a white handkerchief. Mr. Poe was a banker who had been placed in charge of the orphans' care after the fire, and I'm sorry to say that he was extremely prone to error, a phrase which here means "always had a cough, and had placed the three Baudelaire children in an assortment of dangerous positions." The first guardian Mr. Poe found for the youngsters was Count Olaf himself, and the most recent guardian he had found for them was Esmé Squalor, and in between he had placed the children in a variety of circumstances that turned out to be just as unpleasant. This morning they were supposed to learn about their new home, but so far all Mr. Poe had done was have several coughing fits and leave them alone with a poorly written newspaper.

"Good morning, children," Mr. Poe said. "I'm sorry I kept you waiting, but ever since I was promoted to Vice President in Charge of Orphan Affairs I've been very, very busy. Besides, finding you a new home has been something of a chore." He walked over to his desk, which was covered in piles of papers, and sat down in a large chair. "I've put calls in to a variety of distant relatives, but they've heard all about the terrible things that tend to happen wherever you go. Understandably, they're too skittish about Count Olaf to agree to take care of you. 'Skittish' means 'nervous,' by the way. There's one more—"

One of the three telephones on Mr. Poe's desk interrupted him with a loud, ugly ring. "Excuse me," the banker said to the children, and began to speak into the receiver. "Poe here. O.K. O.K. O.K. I thought so. O.K. O.K. Thank you, Mr. Fagin." Mr. Poe hung up the phone and made a mark on one of the papers on his desk. "That was a nineteenth cousin of yours," Mr. Poe said, "and a last hope of mine. I thought I could persuade him to take you in, just for a couple of months, but he refused. I can't say I blame him. I'm concerned that your reputation as troublemakers is even ruining the reputation of my bank."

"But we're not troublemakers," Klaus said.

"Count Olaf is the troublemaker."

Mr. Poe took the newspaper from the children and looked at it carefully. "Well, I'm sure the story in *The Daily Punctilio* will help the authorities finally capture Olaf, and then your relatives will be less skittish."

"But the story is full of mistakes," Violet said. "The authorities won't even know his real name. The newspaper calls him Omar."

"The story was a disappointment to me, too," Mr. Poe said. "The journalist said that the paper would put a photograph of me next to the article, with a caption about my promotion. I had my hair cut for it especially. It would have made my wife and sons very proud to see my name in the papers, so I understand why you're disappointed that the article is about the Quagmire twins, instead of being about you."

"We don't care about having our names in the papers," Klaus said, "and besides, the Quagmires are triplets, not twins."

"The death of their brother changes their

birth identity," Mr. Poe explained sternly, "but I don't have time to talk about this. We need to find—"

Another one of his phones rang, and Mr. Poe excused himself again. "Poe here," he said into the receiver. "No. No. No. Yes. Yes. Yes. I don't *care*. *Good*-bye." He hung up the phone and coughed into his white handkerchief before wiping his mouth and turning once more to the children. "Well, that phone call solved all of your problems," he said simply.

The Baudelaires looked at one another. Had Count Olaf been arrested? Had the Quagmires been saved? Had someone invented a way to go back in time and rescue their parents from the terrible fire? How could all of their problems have been solved with one phone call to a banker?

"Plinn?" Sunny asked.

Mr. Poe smiled. "Have you ever heard the aphorism," he said, "'It takes a village to raise a child'?"

The children looked at one another again, a little less hopefully this time. The quoting of an aphorism, like the angry barking of a dog or the smell of overcooked broccoli, rarely indicates that something helpful is about to happen. An aphorism is merely a small group of words arranged in a certain order because they sound good that way, but oftentimes people tend to say them as if they were saying something very mysterious and wise.

"I know it probably sounds mysterious to you," Mr. Poe continued, "but the aphorism is actually very wise. 'It takes a village to raise a child' means that the responsibility for taking care of youngsters belongs to everyone in the community."

"I think I read something about this aphorism in a book about the Mbuti pygmies," Klaus said. "Are you sending us to live in Africa?"

"Don't be silly," Mr. Poe said, as if the millions of people who lived in Africa were all ridiculous. "That was the city government on the telephone. A number of villages just outside the city have signed up for a new guardian program based on the aphorism 'It takes a village to raise a child.' Orphans are sent to these villages, and everyone who lives there raises them together. Normally, I approve of more traditional family structures, but this is really quite convenient, and your parents' will instructs that you be raised in the most convenient way possible."

"Do you mean that the entire town would be in charge of us?" Violet asked. "That's a lot of people."

"Well, I imagine they would take turns," Mr. Poe said, stroking his chin. "It's not as if you would be tucked into bed by three thousand people at once."

"Snoita!" Sunny shrieked. She meant something like "I prefer to be tucked into bed by my siblings, not by strangers!" but Mr. Poe was busy looking through his papers on his desk and didn't answer her.

"Apparently I was mailed a brochure about this program several weeks ago," he said, "but I guess it got lost somewhere on my desk. Oh, here it is. Take a look for yourselves."

Mr. Poe reached across his desk to hand them a colorful brochure, and the Baudelaire orphans took a look for themselves. On the front was the aphorism 'It takes a village to raise a child' written in flowery letters, and inside the brochure were photographs of children with such huge smiles that the Baudelaires' mouths ached just to look at them. A few paragraphs explained that 99 percent of the orphans participating in this program were overjoyed to have whole villages taking care of them, and that all the towns listed on the back page were eager to serve as guardians for any interested children who had lost their parents. The three Baudelaires looked at the grinning photographs and read the flowery aphorism and felt a little flutter in their stomachs. They felt more than a little nervous about having a whole town for a guardian. It was strange enough when they were in the care of various relatives. How strange would it feel if hundreds of people were trying to act as substitute Baudelaires?

"Do you think we would be safe from Count Olaf," Violet asked hesitantly, "if we lived with an entire village?"

"I should think so," Mr. Poe said, and coughed into his handkerchief. "With a whole village looking after you, you'll probably be the safest you've ever been. Plus, thanks to the story in *The Daily Punctilio*, I'm sure Omar will be captured in no time."

"*Olaf*," Klaus corrected.

"Yes, yes," Mr. Poe said. "I meant to say 'Omar.' Now, what villages are listed in the brochure? You children can choose your new hometown, if you like."

Klaus turned the brochure over and read from the list of towns. "Paltryville," he said. "That's where the Lucky Smells Lumbermill was. We had a terrible time there."

"Calten!" Sunny cried, which meant something like "I wouldn't return there for all the tea in China!"

"The next village on the list is Tedia," Klaus said. "That name is familiar to me."

"That's near where Uncle Monty lived," Violet said. "Let's not live there—it'll make us miss Uncle Monty even more than we already do."

Klaus nodded in agreement. "Besides," he said, "the town is near Lousy Lane, so it probably smells like horseradish. Here's a village I've never heard of—Ophelia."

"No, no," Mr. Poe said. "I won't have you living in the same town as the Ophelia Bank. It's one of my least favorite banks, and I don't want to have to walk by it when I visit you."

"Zounce!" Sunny said, which meant "That's ridiculous!" but Klaus nudged her with his elbow and pointed to the next village listed on the brochure, and Sunny quickly changed her tune, a phrase which here means "immediately said 'Gounce!' instead, which meant something along the lines of 'Let's live there!'"

"Gounce indeed," Klaus agreed, and showed Violet what he and Sunny were talking about. Violet gasped, and the three siblings looked at one another and felt a little flutter in their stomachs again. But this was less of a nervous flutter and more of a hopeful one—a hope that maybe Mr. Poe's last phone call really had solved all their problems, and that maybe what they read right here in the brochure would turn out to be more important than what they didn't read in the newspaper. For at the bottom of the list of villages, below Paltryville and Tedia and Ophelia, was the most important thing they had read all morning. Printed in the flowery script, on the back page of the brochure Mr. Poe had given them, were the letters V.F.D.

Two

When you are traveling by bus, it is always difficult to decide whether you should sit in a seat by the window, a seat on the aisle, or a seat in the middle. If you take an aisle seat, you have the advantage of being able to stretch your legs whenever you like, but you have the disadvantage of people walking by you, and they can accidentally step on your toes or spill something on your clothing. If you take a window seat, you have the advantage of getting a clear view of the scenery, but you have the disadvantage of watching insects die as they hit the glass. If you take a middle seat, you have neither of these advantages, and you have the added disadvantage of people leaning all over you when they fall asleep. You can see at once why you should always arrange to hire a limousine or rent a mule rather than take the bus to your destination.

The Baudelaire orphans, however, did not have the money to hire a limousine, and it would have taken them several weeks to reach V.F.D. by mule, so they were traveling to their new home by bus. The children had thought that it might take a lot of effort to convince Mr. Poe to choose V.F.D. as their new village guardian, but right when they saw the three initials on the brochure, one of Mr. Poe's telephones rang, and by the time he was off the phone he was too busy to argue. All he had time to do was make arrangements with the city government and take them to the bus station. As he saw them off—a phrase which here means "put the Baudelaires on a bus, rather than doing the polite thing and taking them to their new home personally"—he instructed them to report to the Town Hall of V.F.D., and made them promise not to do anything that would ruin his bank's reputation. Before they knew it, Violet was sitting in an aisle seat, brushing dirt off her coat and rubbing her sore toes, and Klaus was sitting in a window seat gazing at the scenery through a layer of dead bugs. Sunny sat between them, gnawing on the armrest.

"No lean!" she said sternly, and her brother smiled.

"Don't worry, Sunny," he said. "We'll make sure not to lean on you if we fall asleep. We don't have much time for napping, anyway—we should be at V.F.D. any minute now."

"What do you think it could stand for?" Violet asked. "Neither the brochure nor the map at the bus station showed anything more than the three initials."

"I don't know," Klaus said. "Do you think we should have told Mr. Poe about the V.F.D. secret? Maybe he could have helped us."

"I doubt it," Violet said. "He hasn't been

very helpful before. I wish the Quagmires were here. I bet they could help us."

"I wish the Quagmires were here even if they couldn't help us," Klaus said, and his sisters nodded in agreement. No Baudelaire had to say anything more about how worried they were about the triplets, and they sat in silence for the rest of the ride, hoping that their arrival at V.F.D. would bring them closer to saving their friends.

"V.F.D.!" the bus driver finally called out. "Next stop V.F.D.! If you look out the window, you can see the town coming up, folks!"

"What does it look like?" Violet asked Klaus.

Klaus peered out the window past the layer of dead bugs. "Flat," he said.

Violet and Sunny leaned over to look and saw that their brother had spoken the truth. The countryside looked as if someone had drawn the line of the horizon—the word "horizon" here means "the boundary where the sky ends and the world begins"—and then forgot to draw in anything else. The land stretched out as far as the eye could see, but there was nothing for the eye to look at but flat, dry land and the occasional sheet of newspaper stirred up by the passing of the bus.

"I don't see any town at all," Klaus said. "Do you suppose it's underground?"

"Novedri!" Sunny said, which meant "Living underground would be no fun at all!"

"Maybe that's the town over there," Violet said, squinting to try and see as far as she could. "You see? Way out by the horizon line, there's a hazy black blur. It looks like smoke, but maybe it's just some buildings seen from far away."

"I can't see it," Klaus said. "That smushed moth is blocking it, I think. But a hazy blur could just be fata morgana."

"Fata?" Sunny asked.

"Fata morgana is when your eyes play tricks on you, particularly in hot weather," Klaus explained. "It's caused by the distortion of light through alternate layers of hot and cool air. It's also called a mirage, but I like the name 'fata morgana' better."

"Me too," Violet agreed, "but let's hope it's not a mirage or fata morgana. Let's hope it's V.F.D."

"V.F.D.!" the bus driver called, as the bus came to a stop. "V.F.D.! Everyone off for V.F.D.!"

The Baudelaires stood up, gathered their belongings, and walked down the aisle, but when they reached the open door of the bus they stopped and stared doubtfully out at the flat and empty landscape.

"Is this really the stop for V.F.D.?" Violet asked the driver. "I thought V.F.D. was a town."

"It is," the driver replied. "Just walk toward that hazy black blur out there on the horizon. I know it looks like—well, I can't remember the phrase for when your eyes play tricks on you—but it's really the town."

"Couldn't you take us a little closer?" Violet asked shyly. "We have a baby with us, and it looks like a long way to walk."

"I wish I could help you," the bus driver said kindly, looking down at Sunny, "but the Council of Elders has very strict rules. I have to let off all passengers for V.F.D. right here; otherwise I could be severely punished."

"Who are the Council of Elders?" Klaus asked.

"Hey!" a voice called from the back of the bus. "Tell those kids to hurry up and get off the bus! The open door is letting bugs in!"

"Off you go, kids," the bus driver said, and the Baudelaires stepped out of the bus onto the flat land of V.F.D. The doors shut, and with a little wave the bus driver drove off and left the children alone on the empty landscape. The siblings watched the bus get smaller and smaller as it drove away, and then turned toward the hazy black blur of their new home.

"Well, now I can see it," Klaus said, squinting behind his glasses, "but I can't believe it. It's going to take the rest of the afternoon to walk all that way."

"Then we'd better get started," Violet said, hoisting Sunny up on top of her suitcase. "This piece of luggage has wheels," she said to her sister, "so you can sit on top of it and I can pull you along."

"Sanks!" Sunny said, which meant "That's very considerate of you!" and the Baudelaires began their long walk toward the hazy black blur on the horizon. After even the first few steps, the disadvantages of the bus ride seemed like small potatoes. "Small potatoes" is a phrase which has nothing to do with root vegetables that happen to be tiny in size. Instead, it refers to the change in one's feelings for something when it is compared with something else. If you were walking in the rain, for instance, you might be worried about getting wet, but if you turned the corner and saw a pack of vicious dogs, getting wet would suddenly become small potatoes next to getting chased down an alley and barked at, or possibly eaten. As the Baudelaires began their long journey toward V.F.D., dead bugs, stepped-on toes, and the possibility of someone leaning on them became small potatoes next to the far more unpleasant things they were encountering. Without anything else on the flat land to blow up against, the wind concentrated its efforts on Violet, a phrase which here means that before long her hair was so wildly tangled that it looked like it had never seen a comb. Because Klaus was standing behind Violet, the wind didn't blow on him much, but without anything else in the empty landscape to cling to, the dust on the ground concentrated its efforts on the middle Baudelaire, and soon he was dusty from head to toe, as if it had been years since he'd had a shower. Perched on top of Violet's luggage, Sunny was out of the way of the dust, but without anything else in the desolate terrain to shine on, the sun concentrated its efforts on her, which meant that she was soon as sunburned as a baby who had spent six months at the seashore, instead of a few hours on top of a suitcase.

But even as they approached the town, V.F.D. still looked as hazy as it did from far away. As the children drew closer and closer to their new home, they could see a number of buildings of different heights and widths, separated by streets both narrow and wide, and the Baudelaires could even see the tall skinny shapes of lampposts and flagpoles stretching out toward the sky. But everything they saw—from the tip of the highest building to the curve of the narrowest street—was pitch black, and seemed to be shaking slightly, as if the entire town were painted on a piece of cloth that was trembling in the wind. The buildings were trembling, and the lampposts were trembling, and even the very streets were shaking ever so slightly, and it was like no town the three Baudelaires had ever seen. It was a mystery, but unlike most mysteries, once the children reached the outskirts of V.F.D. and learned what was causing the trembling effect, they did not feel any better to have the mystery solved.

The town was covered in crows. Nearly every inch of nearly every object had a large black bird roosting on it and casting a suspicious eye on the children as they stood at the very edge of the village. There were crows sitting on the roofs of all the buildings, perching on the windowsills, and squatting on the steps and on the sidewalks. Crows were covering all of the trees, from the very top branches to the roots poking out of the crow-covered ground, and were gathered in large groups on the streets for crow conversations. Crows were covering the lampposts and flagpoles, and there were crows lying down in the gutters and resting between fence posts. There were even six crows crowded together on the sign that read "Town Hall," with an arrow leading down a crow-covered street. The crows weren't squawking or cawing, which is what crows often do, or playing the trumpet, which crows practically never do, but the town was far from silent. The air was filled with the sounds the crows made as they moved around. Sometimes one crow would fly from one perch to another, as if it had suddenly become bored roosting on the mailbox and thought it might be more fun to perch on the doorknob of a building. Occasionally, several crows would flutter their wings, as if they were stiff from sitting together on a bench and wanted to stretch a little bit. And almost constantly, the crows would shift in their places, trying to make themselves as comfortable as they could in such cramped quarters. All this motion explained why the town had looked so shivery in the distance, but it certainly didn't make the Baudelaires feel any better, and they stood together in silence for quite some time, trying to find the courage to walk among all the fluttering black birds.

"I've read three books on crows," Klaus said. "They're perfectly harmless."

"Yes, I know," Violet said. "It's unusual to see so many crows in one place, but they're nothing to worry about. It's small potatoes."

"Zimuster," Sunny agreed, but the three children still did not take a step closer to the crow-covered town. Despite what they had said to one another—that the crows were harmless birds, that they had nothing to worry about, and "Zimuster," which meant something along the lines of "It would be silly to be afraid of a bunch of birds"—the Baudelaires felt they were encountering some very large potatoes indeed.

If I had been one of the Baudelaires myself, I would have stood at the edge of town for the rest of my life, whimpering with fear, rather than take even one step into the crow-covered streets, but it only took the Baudelaires a few minutes to work up the courage to walk through all of the muttering, scuffling birds to Town Hall.

"This isn't as difficult as I thought it might be," Violet said, in a quiet voice so as not to disturb the crows closest to her. "It's not exactly small potatoes, but there's enough space between the groups of crows to step."

"That's true," Klaus said, his eyes on the

sidewalk to avoid stepping on any crow tails. "And they tend to move aside, just a little bit, as we walk by."

"Racah," Sunny said, crawling as carefully as she could. She meant something along the lines of "It's almost like walking through a quiet, but polite, crowd of very short people," and her siblings smiled in agreement. Before too long, they had walked the entire block of the crow-lined street, and there at the far corner was a tall, impressive building that appeared to be made of white marble—at least, as far as the Baudelaires could tell, because it was as covered with crows as the rest of the neighborhood. Even the sign reading "Town Hall" looked like it read "wn Ha," because three enormous crows were perched on it, gazing at the Baudelaires with their tiny beady eyes. Violet raised her hand as if to knock on the door, but then paused.

"What's the matter?" Klaus said.

"Nothing," Violet replied, but her hand still

hung in the air. "I guess I'm just a little skittish. After all, this is the Town Hall of V.F.D. For all we know, behind this door may be the secret we've been looking for since the Quagmires were first kidnapped."

"Maybe we shouldn't get our hopes up," Klaus said. "Remember, when we lived with the Squalors, we thought we had solved the V.F.D. mystery, but we were wrong. We could be wrong this time, too."

"But we could be right," Violet said, "and if we're right, we should be prepared for whatever terrible thing is behind this door."

"Unless we're wrong," Klaus pointed out. "Then we have nothing to be prepared for."

"Gaksoo!" Sunny said. She meant something along the lines of "There's no point in arguing, because we'll never know whether we're right or wrong until we knock on the door," and before her siblings could answer her she crawled around Klaus's legs and took the plunge, a phrase which here means "knocked firmly on the door with her tiny knuckles."

"Come in!" called a very grand voice, and the Baudelaires opened the door and found themselves in a large room with a very high ceiling, a very shiny floor, and a very long bench, with very detailed portraits of crows hanging on the walls. In front of the bench was a small platform where a woman in a motorcycle helmet was standing, and behind the platform were perhaps one hundred folding chairs, most of which had a person sitting on them who was staring at the Baudelaire orphans. But the Baudelaire orphans were not staring back. The three children were staring so hard at the people sitting on the bench that they scarcely glanced at the folding chairs at all.

On the bench, sitting stiffly side by side, were twenty-five people who had two things in common. The first thing was that they were all quite old—the youngest person on the bench, a woman sitting on the far end, looked about eighty-one years of age, and everyone else looked quite a bit older. But the second thing they had in common was far more interesting. At first glance it looked like a few crows had flown in from the streets and roosted on the bench-sitters' heads, but as the Baudelaires looked more closely, they saw that the crows did not blink their eyes, or flutter their wings or move at all in any way, and the children realized that they were nothing more than black hats, made in such a way as to resemble actual crows. It was such a strange kind of hat to be wearing that the children found themselves staring for quite a few minutes without noticing anything else.

"Are you the Baudelaire orphans?" asked one of the old men who was sitting on the bench, in a gravelly voice. As he talked, his crow head flapped slightly, which only made it look more ridiculous. "We've been expecting you, although I wasn't told you would look so terrible. You three are the most windswept, dusty, and sunburned children I have ever seen. Are you sure you're the children we've been waiting for?"

"Yes," Violet replied. "I'm Violet Baude-laire, and this is my brother, Klaus, and my sister, Sunny, and the reason why we—"

"Shush," one of the other old men said. "We're not discussing you right now. Rule #492 clearly states that the Council of Elders will only discuss things that are on the platform. Right now we are discussing our new Chief of Police. Are there any questions from the townspeople regarding Officer Luciana?"

"Yes, I have a question," called out a man in plaid pants. "I want to know what happened to our previous Chief of Police. I liked that guy."

The woman on the platform held up a white-gloved hand, and the Baudelaires turned to look at her for the first time. Officer Luciana was a very tall woman wearing big black boots, a blue coat with a shiny badge, and a motorcycle helmet with the visor pulled down to cover her eyes. The Baudelaires could see her mouth, below the edge of the visor, covered in bright red lipstick. "The previous Chief of Police has a sore throat," she said, turning her helmet to the man who had asked the question. "He accidentally swallowed a box of thumbtacks. But let's not waste time talking about him. I am your new Chief of Police, and I will make sure that any rulebreakers in town are punished properly. I can't see how there's anything more to discuss."

"I quite agree with you," said the first Elder who had spoken, as the people in folding chairs nodded. "The Council of Elders hereby ends the discussion of Officer Luciana. Hector, please bring the orphans to the platform for discussion."

A tall skinny man in rumpled overalls stood up from one of the folding chairs as the Chief of Police stepped off the platform with a lipsticked smile on. His eyes on the floor, the man walked over to the Baudelaires and pointed first at the Council of Elders sitting on the bench and then at the empty platform. Although they would have preferred a more polite method of communication, the children understood at once, and Violet and Klaus stepped up onto the platform and then lifted Sunny up to join them.

One of the women in the Council of Elders spoke up. "We are now discussing the guardianship of the Baudelaire orphans. Under the new government program, the entire town of V.F.D. will act as guardian over these three children because it takes a village to raise a child. Are there any questions?"

"Are these the same Baudelaires," came a voice from the back of the room, "who are involved in the kidnapping of the Quagmire twins by Count Omar?"

The Baudelaires turned around to see a woman dressed in a bright pink bathrobe and holding up a copy of *The Daily Punctilio*. "It says here in the newspaper that an evil count is coming after those children. I don't want someone like that in our town!"

"We've taken care of that matter, Mrs. Morrow," replied another member of the Council soothingly. "We'll explain in a moment. Now, when children have a guardian, the guardian makes them do chores, so it follows that you Baudelaires will do all the chores for the entire village. Beginning tomorrow, you three children will be responsible for anything that anyone asks you to do."

The children looked at each other in disbelief. "Begging your pardon," Klaus said timidly, "but there are only twenty-four hours in a day, and there appear to be several hundred townspeople. How will we find the time to do everyone's chores?"

"Hush!" several members of the Council said in unison, and then the youngest-looking woman spoke up. "Rule #920 clearly states that no one may talk while on the platform unless you are a police officer. You're orphans, not police officers, so shut up. Now, due to the V.F.D. crows, you will have to arrange your chore schedule as follows: In the morning, the crows roost uptown, so that's when you will do all the downtown chores, so the crows don't get in your way. In the afternoon, as you can see, the crows roost downtown, so you will do the uptown chores then. Please pay particular attention to our new fountàin, which was just installed this morning. It's very beautiful, and needs to be kept as clean as possible. At night, the crows roost in Nevermore Tree, which is on the outskirts of town, so there's no problem there. Are there any questions?"

"I have a question," said the man in plaid pants. He stood up from his folding chair and pointed at the Baudelaires. "Where are they going to live? It may take a village to raise a child, but that doesn't mean that our homes have to be disturbed by noisy children, does it?"

"Yes," agreed Mrs. Morrow. "I'm all for the orphans doing our chores, but I don't want them cluttering up my house."

Several other townspeople spoke up. "Hear, hear!" they said, using an expression which here means "I don't want Violet, Klaus, and Sunny Baudelaire to live with me, either!"

One of the oldest-looking Elders raised both his hands up in the air. "Please," he said. "There is no reason for all this fuss. The children will live with Hector, our handyman. He will feed them, clothe them, and make sure they do all the chores, and he is responsible for teaching them all of the rules of V.F.D., so they won't do any more terrible things, such as talking while on the platform."

"Thank goodness for that," muttered the man in plaid pants.

"Now, Baudelaires," said yet another member of the Council. She was sitting so far from the platform that she had to crane her head to look at the children, and her hat looked like it would fall off her head. "Before Hector takes you to his house, I'm sure you have some concerns of your own. It's too bad you're not allowed to speak right now, otherwise you could tell us what they were. But Mr. Poe sent us some materials regarding this Count Olaf person."

"Omar," corrected Mrs. Morrow, pointing to the headline in the newspaper.

"Silence!" the Elder said. "Now, Baudelaires, I'm sure you are very concerned about this Olaf fellow, but as your guardian, the town will protect you. That is why we have recently made up a new rule, Rule #19,833. It clearly states that no villains are allowed within the city limits."

"Hear, hear!" the townspeople cried, and the Council of Elders nodded in appreciation, bobbing their crow-shaped hats.

"Now, if there are no more questions," an Elder concluded, "Hector, please take the Baudelaires off the platform and take them to your house."

Still keeping his eyes on the floor, the man in overalls strode silently to the platform and led them out of the room. The children hurried to catch up with the handyman, who had not said one word all this time. Was he unhappy to be taking care of three children? Was he angry at the Council of Elders? Was he unable to speak at all? It reminded the Baudelaires of one of Count Olaf's associates, the one who looked like neither a man nor a woman and who never seemed to speak. The children kept a few steps behind Hector as he walked out of the building, almost afraid to get any closer to a man who was so strange and silent.

When Hector opened the door of Town Hall and led the children back out onto the crow-covered sidewalk, he let out a big sigh—the first sound the children had heard from him. Then he looked down at each Baudelaire and gave them a gentle smile. "I'm never truly relaxed," he said to them in a pleasant voice, "until I have left Town Hall. The Council of Elders makes me feel very skittish. All those strict rules! It make me so skittish that I never speak during one of their council meetings. But I always feel much better the moment I walk out of the building. Now, it looks like we're going to be spending quite a bit of time together, so let's get a few things straight. Number one, call me Hector. Number two, I hope you like Mexican food, because that's my specialty. And number three, I want you to see something marvelous, and we're just in time. The sun is starting to set."

It was true. The Baudelaires hadn't noticed, when they stepped out of Town Hall, that the afternoon light had slipped away and that the sun was now just beginning to dip below the horizon. "It's lovely," Violet said politely, although she had never understood all the fuss about standing around admiring sunsets.

"Shh," Hector said. "Who cares about the sunset? Just be quiet for a minute, and watch the crows. It should happen any second now."

"What should happen?" Klaus said.

"Shh," Hector said again, and then it began to happen. The Council of Elders had already told the Baudelaires about the roosting habits of the crows, but the three children hadn't really given the matter a second thought, a phrase which here means "considered, even for a second, what it would look like when thousands of crows would fly together to a new location." One of the largest crows, sitting on top of the mailbox, was the first to fly up in the air, and with a rustle of wings he—or she; it was hard to tell from so far away—began to fly in a large circle over the children's heads. Then a crow from one of Town Hall's windowsills flew up to join the first crow, and then one from a nearby bush, and then three from the street, and then hundreds of crows began to rise up at once and circle in the air, and it was as if an enormous shadow was being lifted from the town. The Baudelaires could finally see what all the streets looked like, and they could gaze at each detail of the buildings as more and more crows left their afternoon roosts. But the children scarcely looked at the town. Instead they looked straight up, at the mysterious and beautiful sight of all those birds making a huge circle in the sky.

"Isn't it marvelous?" Hector cried. His long skinny arms were outstretched, and he had to raise his voice over the sound of all the fluttering wings. "Isn't it marvelous?"

Violet, Klaus, and Sunny nodded in agreement, and stared at the thousands of crows circling and circling above them like a mass of fluttering smoke or like black, fresh ink—such as the ink I am using now, to write down these events—that somehow had found its way to the heavens. The sound of the wings sounded like a million pages being flipped, and the wind from all that fluttering blew in their grinning faces. For a moment, with all that air rushing toward them, the Baudelaire orphans felt as if they too could fly up into the air, away from Count Olaf and all their troubles, and join the circle of crows in the evening sky.

Three

"*Wasn't* that marvelous?" Hector said, as the crows stopped circling and began to fly, like an enormous black cloud, over the buildings and away from the Baudelaire orphans. "Wasn't that just marvelous? Wasn't that absolutely superlative? That means the same thing as 'marvelous,' by the way."

"It certainly was," Klaus agreed, not adding that he had known the word "superlative" since he was eleven.

"I see that just about every evening," Hector said, "and it always impresses me. It always makes me hungry, too. What shall we eat this evening? How about chicken enchiladas? That's a Mexican dish consisting of corn tortillas rolled around a chicken filling, covered with melted cheese and a special sauce I learned from my second-grade teacher. How does that sound?"

"That sounds delicious," Violet said.

"Oh, good," Hector said. "I despise picky eaters. Well, it's a pretty long walk to my house, so let's talk as we go. Here, I'll carry your suit-cases and you two can carry your sister. I know you had to walk from the bus stop, so she's had more than enough exercise for a baby."

Hector grabbed the Baudelaires' bags and led the way down the street, which was now empty except for a few stray crow feathers. High above their heads, the crows were taking a sharp left-hand turn, and Hector raised Klaus's suit-case to point at them. "I don't know if you're familiar with the expression 'as the crow flies,'" Hector said, "but it means 'the most direct route.' If something is a mile away as the crow flies, that means it's the shortest way to get there. It usually has nothing to do with actual crows, but in this case it does. We're about a mile away from my home as the crow flies—as all those crows fly, as a matter of fact. At night, they roost in Nevermore Tree, which is in my backyard. But it takes us longer to get there, of course, because we have to walk through V.F.D. instead of flying up in the air."

"Hector," Violet said timidly, "we were wondering exactly what V.F.D. stands for."

"Oh yes," Klaus said. "Please tell us."

"Of course I'll tell you," Hector said, "but I don't know why you're so excited about it. It's just more nonsense from the Council of Elders."

The Baudelaires looked at one another uncertainly. "What do you mean?" Klaus asked.

"Well, about three hundred and six years ago," Hector said, "a group of explorers discovered the murder of crows that we just saw."

"Sturo?" Sunny asked.

"We didn't see any crows get killed," Violet said.

"'Murder' is the word for a group of crows, like a flock of geese or a herd of cows or a convention of orthodontists. Anyway, the explorers were impressed with their patterns of migration—you know, they always fly uptown in the morning, downtown in the afternoon and over to Nevermore Tree in the evening. It's a very unusual pattern, and the explorers were so excited by it that they decided to live here. Before too long, a town sprung up, and so they named it V.F.D."

"But what does V.F.D. stand for?" Violet asked.

"The Village of Fowl Devotees," Hector said. "'Devotees' is a word for people who are devoted to something, and 'fowl'—"

"—means 'bird,'" Klaus finished. "That's the secret of V.F.D.? Village of Fowl Devotees?"

"What do you mean, secret?" Hector asked. "It's not a secret. Everyone knows what those letters mean."

The Baudelaires sighed with confusion and dismay, which is not a pleasant combination. "What my brother means," Violet explained, "is that we chose V.F.D. to become our new guardian because we'd been told of a terrible secret—a secret with the initials V.F.D."

"Who told you about this secret?" Hector asked.

"Some very dear friends of ours," Violet replied. "Duncan and Isadora Quagmire. They discovered something about Count Olaf, but before they could tell us anything more—"

"Hold on a minute," Hector said. "Who's Count Olaf? Mrs. Morrow was talking about Count *Omar*. Is Olaf his brother?"

"No," Klaus said, shuddering at the very thought of Olaf having a brother. "I'm afraid *The Daily Punctilio* got many of the facts wrong."

"Well, why don't we get them right," Hector said, turning a corner. "Suppose you tell me exactly what happened."

"It's sort of a long story," Violet said.

"Well," Hector said, with a slight smile, "we have sort of a long walk. Why don't you begin at the beginning?"

The Baudelaires looked up at Hector, sighed, and began at the beginning, which seemed such a long way off that they were surprised they could remember it so clearly. Violet told Hector about the dreadful day at the beach when she and her siblings learned from Mr. Poe that their parents had been killed in the fire that had destroyed their home, and Klaus told Hector about the days they spent in Count Olaf's care. Sunny—with some help from Klaus and Violet, who translated for her—told him about poor Uncle Monty, and about the terrible things that had happened to Aunt Josephine. Violet told Hector about working at Lucky Smells Lumbermill, and Klaus told him about enrolling at Prufrock Preparatory School, and Sunny related the dismal time they had living with Jerome and Esmé Squalor at 667 Dark Avenue. Violet told Hector all about Count Olaf's various disguises, and about each and every one of his nefarious associates, including the hook-handed man, the two powder-faced women, the bald man with the long nose, and the one who looked like neither a man nor a woman, of whom the Baudelaires had been reminded when Hector had been so silent. Klaus told Hector all about the Quagmire triplets, and about the mysterious underground passageway that had led back to their home, and about the shadow of misfortune that had seemed to hang over them nearly every moment since that day at the beach. And as the Baudelaires told Hector their long story, they began to feel as if the handyman was carrying more than their suitcases. They felt as if he was carrying each word they said, as if each unfortunate event was a burden that Hector was helping them with. The story of their lives was so miserable that I cannot say they felt happy when they were through telling it, but by the time Sunny concluded the whole long story, the Baudelaires felt as if they were carrying much less.

"Kyun," Sunny concluded, which Violet was quick to translate as "And that's why we chose this town, in the hopes of finding the secret of V.F.D., rescuing the Quagmire triplets, and defeating Count Olaf once and for all."

Hector sighed. "You've certainly been through an ordeal," he said, using a word which here means "a heap of trouble, most of which was Count Olaf's fault." He stopped for a second and looked at each Baudelaire. "You've been very brave, all three of you, and I'll do my best to make sure you have a proper home with me. But I must tell you that I think you've hit a dead end."

"What do you mean?" Klaus asked.

"Well, I hate to add some bad news to the

terrible story you just told me," Hector said, "but I think the initials that the Quagmires told you about and the initials of this town are just a coincidence. As I said, this village has been called V.F.D. for more than three hundred years. Scarcely anything has changed since then. The crows have always roosted in the same places. The meetings of the Council of Elders have always been at the same time every day. My father was the handyman before me, and his father was the handyman before him, and so on and so on. The only new things in this town are you three children and the new Fowl Fountain uptown, which we'll be cleaning tomorrow. I don't see how this village could have anything to do with the secret the Quagmires discovered."

The Baudelaire children looked at one another in frustration. "Pojik?" Sunny asked in exasperation. She meant something along the lines of "Do you mean we've come here for nothing?" but Violet translated it somewhat differently.

"What my sister means," Violet said, "is that it's very frustrating to find that we're in the wrong place."

"We're very concerned for our friends," Klaus added, "and we don't want to give up on finding them."

"Give up?" Hector said. "Who said anything about giving up? Just because the name of this town isn't helpful, that doesn't mean you're in the wrong place. We obviously have a great many chores to do, but in our spare time we can try to find out the whereabouts of Duncan and Isadora. I'm a handyman, not a detective, but I'll try to help you the best I can. We'll have to be very careful, though. The Council of Elders has so many rules that you can scarcely do anything without breaking one of them."

"Why does the Council have so many rules?" Violet asked.

"Why does anyone have a lot of rules?" Hector said with a shrug. "So they can boss people around, I guess. Thanks to all the rules of V.F.D., the Council of Elders can tell people what to wear, how to talk, what to eat, and even what to build. Rule #67, for instance, clearly states that no citizen is allowed to build or use any mechanical devices."

"Does that mean I can't build or use any mechanical devices?" Violet asked Hector. "Are my siblings and I citizens of V.F.D., now that the town is our guardian?"

"I'm afraid you are," Hector said. "You have to follow Rule #67, along with all the other rules."

"But Violet's an inventor!" Klaus cried. "Mechanical devices are very important to her!"

"Is that so?" Hector said, and smiled. "Then you can be a very big help to me, Violet." He stopped walking, and looked around the street as if it was full of spies, instead of being completely empty. "Can you keep a secret?" he asked.

"Yes," Violet answered.

Hector looked around the street once more,

and then leaned forward and began speaking in a very quiet voice. "When the Council of Elders invented Rule #67," he said, "they instructed me to remove all the inventing materials in town."

"What did you say?" Klaus asked.

"I didn't say anything," Hector admitted, leading the children around another corner. "The Council makes me too skittish to speak; you know that. But here's what I did. I took all of the materials and hid them out in my barn, which I've been using as sort of an inventing studio."

"I've always wanted to have an inventing studio," Violet said. Without even realizing it, she was reaching into her pocket for a ribbon, to tie her hair up and keep it out of her eyes, as if she were already inventing something instead of just talking about it. "What have you invented so far, Hector?"

"Oh, just a few little things," Hector said, "but I have an enormous project that is nearing completion. I've been building a self-sustaining hot air mobile home."

"Neebdes?" Sunny said. She meant something like, "Could you explain that a bit more?" but Hector needed no encouragement to keep talking about his invention.

"I don't know if you've ever been up in a hot air balloon," he said, "but it's very exciting. You stand in a large basket, with the enormous balloon over your head, and you can gaze down at the entire countryside below you, spread out like a blanket. It's simply superlative. Well, my invention is nothing more than a hot air balloon—except it's much larger. Instead of one large basket, there are twelve baskets, all tied together below several hot air balloons. Each basket serves as a different room, so it's like having an entire flying house. It's completely self-sustaining—once you get up in it, you never have to go back down. In fact, if my new engine works properly, it will be impossible to get back down. The engine should last for more than one hundred years, and there's a huge storage basket that I'm filling with food, beverages, clothing, and books. Once it's completed, I'll be able to fly away from V.F.D. and the Council of Elders and everything else that makes me skittish, and live forever in the air."

"It sounds like a marvelous invention," Violet said. "How in the world have you been able to get the engine to be self-sustaining, too?"

"That's giving me something of a problem," Hector admitted, "but maybe if you three took a look at it, we could fix the engine together."

"I'm sure Violet could be of help," Klaus said, "but I'm not much of an inventor. I'm more interested in reading. Does V.F.D. have a good library?"

"Unfortunately, no," Hector said. "Rule #108 clearly states that the V.F.D. library cannot contain any books that break any of the other rules. If someone in a book uses a mechanical device, for instance, that book is not allowed in the library."

"But there are so many rules," Klaus said. "What kind of books could possibly be allowed?"

"Not very many," Hector said, "and nearly all of them are dull. There's one called *The Littlest Elf* that's probably the most boring book ever written. It's about this irritating little man who has all sorts of tedious adventures."

"That's too bad," Klaus said glumly. "I was hoping that I could do a little research into V.F.D.—the secret, that is, not the village—in my spare time."

Hector stopped walking again, and looked once more around the empty streets. "Can you keep another secret?" he asked, and the Baudelaires nodded. "The Council of Elders told me to burn all of the books that broke Rule #108," he said in a quiet voice, "but I brought them to my barn instead. I have sort of a secret library there, as well as a secret inventing studio."

"Wow," Klaus said. "I've seen public libraries, private libraries, school libraries, legal libraries, reptile libraries, and grammatical libraries, but never a secret library. It sounds exciting."

"It's a bit exciting," Hector agreed, "but it also makes me very skittish. The Council of Elders gets very, very angry when people break the rules. I hate to think what they'd do to me if they found out I was secretly using mechanical devices and reading interesting books."

"Azzator!" Sunny said, which meant "Don't worry—your secret is safe with us!"

Hector looked down at her quizzically. "I don't know what 'azzator' means, Sunny," he said, "but I would guess it means 'Don't forget about me!' Violet will use the studio, and Klaus will use the library, but what can we do for you? What do you like to do best?"

"Bite!" Sunny responded at once, but Hector frowned and took another look around him.

"Don't say that so loudly, Sunny!" he whispered. "Rule #4,561 clearly states that citizens are not allowed to use their mouths for recreation. If the Council of Elders knew that you liked to bite things for your own enjoyment, I can't imagine what they'd do. I'm sure we can find you some things to bite, but you'll have to do it in secret. Well, here we are."

Hector led the Baudelaires around one last corner, and the children got their first glimpse of where they would be living. The street they had been walking on simply ended at the turn of the corner, leading them to a place as wide and as flat as the countryside they had crossed that afternoon, with just three shapes standing out on the flat horizon. The first was a large, sturdy-looking house, with a pointed roof and a front porch big enough to contain a picnic table and four wooden chairs. The second was an enormous barn, right next to the house, that hid the studio and library Hector had been talking about. But it was the third shape that caused the Baudelaires to stare.

The third shape on the horizon was Nevermore Tree, but to simply say it was a tree would be like saying the Pacific Ocean was a body of water, or that Count Olaf was a grumpy person or that the story of Beatrice and myself was just a little bit sad. Nevermore Tree was gargantuan, a word which here means "having attained an inordinate amount of botanical volume," a phrase which here means "it was the biggest tree the Baudelaires had ever seen." Its trunk was so wide that the Baudelaires could have stood behind it, along with an elephant, three horses, and an opera singer, and not have been seen from the other side. Its branches spread out in every direction, like a fan that was taller than the house and wider than the barn, and the tree was made even taller and wider by what was sitting in it. Every last V.F.D. crow was roosting in its branches, adding a thick layer of muttering black shapes to the immense silhouette of the tree. Because the crows had gotten to Hector's house as the crow flies, instead of walking, the birds had arrived long before the Baudelaires, and the air was filled with the quiet rustling sounds of the birds settling in for the evening. A few of the birds had already fallen asleep, and the children could hear a few crow snores as they approached their new home.

"What do you think?" Hector asked.

"It's marvelous," Violet said.

"It's superlative," Klaus said.

"Ogufod!" Sunny said, which meant "What a lot of crows!"

"The noises of the crows might sound strange at first," Hector said, leading the way up the steps of the house, "but you'll get used to them before long. I always leave the windows open when I go to bed. The sounds of the crows remind me of the ocean, and I find it very peaceful to listen to them as I drift off to sleep. Speaking of bed, I'm sure you must be very tired. I've prepared three rooms for you upstairs, but if you don't like them you can choose other ones. There's plenty of room in the house. There's even room for the Quagmires to live here, when we find them. It sounds like the five of you would be happy living together, even if you had to do the chores of an entire town."

"That sounds delightful," Violet said, smiling at Hector. It made the children happy just to think of the two triplets being safe and sound, instead of in Count Olaf's clutches. "Duncan is a journalist, so maybe he could start a newspaper—then V.F.D. wouldn't have to read all of the mistakes in *The Daily Punctilio*."

"And Isadora is a poet," Klaus said. "She could write a book of poetry for the library—as long as she didn't write poetry about things that were against the rules."

Hector started to open the door of his house, but then paused and gave the Baudelaires a strange look. "A poet?" he asked. "What kind of poetry does she write?"

"Couplets," Violet replied.

Hector gave the children a look that was even stranger. He put down the Baudelaires' suitcases and reached into the pocket of his overalls. "Couplets?" he asked.

"Yes," Klaus said. "She likes to write rhyming poems that are two lines long."

Hector gave the youngsters a look that was one of the strangest they had ever seen, and took his hand out of his pocket to show them a scrap of paper rolled into a tiny scroll. "Like this?" he asked, and unrolled the paper. The Baudelaire orphans had to squint to read it in the dying light of the sunset, and when they read it once they had to read it again, to make sure that the light wasn't playing tricks on them and that they had read what was really there on the scrap of paper, in shaky but familiar hand-writing:

For sapphires we are held in here.
Only you can end our fear.

The Baudelaire orphans stared at the scrap of paper, and then at Hector, and then at the scrap of paper again. Then they stared at Hector again, and then at the scrap of paper once more and then at Hector once more and then at the scrap of paper once again, and then at Hector once again and then at the scrap of paper one more time. Their mouths were open as if they were about to speak, but the three children could not find the words they wanted to say.

The expression "a bolt from the blue" describes something so surprising that it makes your head spin, your legs wobble, and your body buzz with astonishment—as if a bolt of lightning suddenly came down from a clear blue sky and struck you at full force. Unless you are a lightbulb, an electrical appliance, or a tree that is tired of standing upright, encountering a bolt from the blue is not a pleasant experience, and for a few minutes the Baudelaires stood on the steps of Hector's house and felt the unpleasant sensations of spinning heads, wobbly legs, and buzzing bodies.

"My goodness, Baudelaires," Hector said. "I've never seen anyone look so surprised. Here, come in the house and sit down. You look like a bolt of lightning just hit you at full force."

The Baudelaires followed Hector into his house and down a hallway to the parlor, where they sat down on a couch without a word. "Why don't you sit here for a few minutes," he said. "I'm going to fix you some hot tea. Maybe by the time it's ready you'll be able to talk." He leaned down and handed the scrap of paper to

Violet, and gave Sunny a little pat on the head before walking out of the parlor and leaving the children alone. Without speaking, Violet unrolled the paper so the siblings could read the couplet again.

> *For sapphires we are held in here.*
> *Only you can end our fear.*

"It's her," Klaus said, speaking quietly so Hector wouldn't hear him. "I'm sure of it. Isadora Quagmire wrote this poem."

"I think so, too," Violet said. "I'm positive it's her handwriting."

"Blake!" Sunny said, which meant "And the poem is written in Isadora's distinct literary style!"

"The poem talks about sapphires," Violet said, "and the triplets' parents left behind the famous Quagmire sapphires when they died."

"Olaf kidnapped them to get ahold of those

sapphires," Klaus said. "That must be what it means when it says 'For sapphires we are held in here.'"

"Peng?" Sunny asked.

"I don't know how Hector got ahold of this," Violet replied. "Let's ask him."

"Not so fast," Klaus said. He took the poem from Violet and looked at it again. "Maybe Hector's involved with the kidnapping in some way."

"I hadn't thought of that," Violet said. "Do you really think so?"

"I don't know," Klaus said. "He doesn't seem like one of Count Olaf's associates, but sometimes we haven't been able to recognize them."

"Wryb," Sunny said thoughtfully, which meant "That's true."

"He seems like someone we can trust," Violet said. "He was excited to show us the migration of the crows, and he wanted to hear all about everything that has happened to us.

That doesn't sound like a kidnapper, but I suppose there's no way of knowing for sure."

"Exactly," Klaus said. "There's no way of knowing for sure."

"The tea's all ready," Hector called from the next room. "If you're up to it, why don't you join me in the kitchen? You can sit at the table while I make the enchiladas."

The Baudelaires looked at one another, and nodded. "Kay!" Sunny called, and led her siblings into a large and cozy kitchen. The children took seats at a round wooden table, where Hector had placed three steaming mugs of tea, and sat quietly while Hector began to prepare dinner. It is true, of course, that there is no way of knowing for sure whether or not you can trust someone, for the simple reason that circumstances change all of the time. You might know someone for several years, for instance, and trust him completely as your friend, but circumstances could change and he could become very hungry, and before you knew it you could be boiling in a soup pot, because there is no way of knowing for sure. I myself fell in love with a wonderful woman who was so charming and intelligent that I trusted that she would be my bride, but there was no way of knowing for sure, and all too soon circumstances changed and she ended up marrying someone else, all because of something she read in *The Daily Punctilio*. And no one had to tell the Baudelaire orphans that there was no way of knowing for sure, because before they became orphans, they lived for many years in the care their parents, and trusted their parents to keep on caring for them, but circumstances changed, and now their parents were dead and the children were living with a handyman in a town full of crows. But even though there is no way of knowing for sure, there are often ways to know for pretty sure, and as the three siblings watched Hector work in the kitchen they spotted some of those ways. The tune he hummed as he chopped the ingredients, for instance, was a comforting one, and the

Baudelaires could not imagine that a person could hum like that if he were a kidnapper. When he saw that the Baudelaires' tea was still too hot to sip, he walked over to the kitchen and blew on each of their mugs to cool it, and it was hard to believe that someone could be hiding two triplets and cooling three children's tea at the same time. And most comforting of all, Hector didn't pester them with a lot of questions about why they were so surprised and silent. He simply kept quiet and let the Baudelaires wait until they were ready to speak about the scrap of paper he had given them, and the children could not imagine that such a considerate person was involved with Count Olaf in any way whatsoever. There was no way of knowing for sure, of course, but as the Baudelaires watched the handyman place the enchiladas in the oven to bake, they felt as if they knew for pretty sure, and by the time he sat down and joined them at the table they were ready to tell him about the couplet they had read.

"This poem was written by Isadora Quagmire," Klaus said without preamble, a phrase which here means "almost as soon as Hector sat down."

"Wow," Hector said. "No wonder you were so surprised. But how can you be sure? Lots of poets write couplets. Ogden Nash, for instance."

"Ogden Nash doesn't write about sapphires," said Klaus, who had received a biography of Ogden Nash for his seventh birthday. "Isadora does. When the Quagmire parents died, they left behind a fortune in sapphires. That's what she means by 'For sapphires we are held in here.'"

"Besides," Violet said, "it's Isadora's handwriting and distinct literary style."

"Well," Hector said, "if you say this poem is by Isadora Quagmire, I believe you."

"We should call Mr. Poe, and tell him," Klaus said.

"We can't call him," Hector said. "There are

no telephones in V.F.D., because telephones are mechanical devices. The Council of Elders can send a message to him. I'm too skittish to ask them, but you can do so if you wish."

"Well, before we talk to the Council, we should know a bit more about the couplet," Violet said. "Where did you get ahold of this scrap of paper?"

"I found it today," Hector said, "beneath the branches of Nevermore Tree. I woke up this morning, and I was just leaving to walk downtown to do the morning chores when I noticed something white among all the black feathers the crows had left behind. It was this scrap of paper, all rolled up in a little scroll. I didn't understand what was written on it, and I needed to get the chores done, so I put it in the pocket of my overalls, and I didn't think of it again until just now, when we were talking about couplets. It's certainly very mysterious. How in the world did one of Isadora's poems end up in my backyard?"

"Well, poems don't get up and walk by themselves," Violet said. "Isadora must have put it here. She must be someplace nearby."

Hector shook his head. "I don't think so," he said. "You saw for yourself how flat it is around here. You can see everything for miles around, and the only things here on the outskirts of town are the house, the barn, and Nevermore Tree. You're welcome to search the house, but you're not going to find Isadora Quagmire or anyone else, and I always keep the barn locked because I don't want the Council of Elders to find out I'm breaking the rules."

"Maybe she's in the tree," Klaus said. "It's certainly big enough that Olaf could hide her in the branches."

"That's true," Violet said. "Last time Olaf was keeping them far below us. Maybe this time they're far above us." She shuddered, thinking of how unpleasant it would be to find yourself trapped in Nevermore Tree's enormous branches, and she pushed her chair back from the table and stood up. "There's only one thing to do," she said. "We'll have to go up and look for them."

"You're right," Klaus said, and stood up beside her. "Let's go."

"Gerhit!" Sunny agreed.

"Hold on a minute," Hector said. "We can't just go climbing up Nevermore Tree."

"Why not?" Violet said. "We've climbed up a tower and down an elevator shaft. Climbing a tree should be no problem."

"I'm sure you three are fine climbers," Hector said, "but that's not what I mean." He stood up and walked over to the kitchen window. "Take a look outside," he said. "The sun has completely set. It's not light enough to see a friend of yours up in Nevermore Tree. Besides, the tree is covered in roosting birds. You'll never be able to climb through all of those crows—it'll be a wild-goose chase."

The Baudelaires looked out the window and saw that Hector was right. The tree was merely an enormous shadow, blurry around the edges where the birds were roosting. The children knew that a climb in such darkness would indeed be a wild-goose chase, a phrase which here means "unlikely to reveal the Quagmires triplets' location." Klaus and Sunny looked at their sister, hoping that she could invent a solution, and were relieved to hear she had thought of something before she could even tie her hair back in a ribbon. "We could climb with flashlights," Violet said. "If you have some tinfoil, an old broom handle, and three rubber bands, I can make a flashlight myself in ten minutes."

Hector shook his head. "Flashlights would only disturb the crows," he said. "If someone woke you up in the middle of the night and shone a light in your face, you would be very annoyed, and you don't want to be surrounded by thousands of annoyed crows. It's better to wait until morning, when the crows have migrated uptown."

"We can't wait until morning," Klaus said.

"We can't wait another second. The last time we found them, we left them alone for a few minutes, and then they were gone again."

"Ollawmove!" Sunny shrieked, which meant "Olaf could move them at any time!"

"Well, he can't move them now," Hector pointed out. "It would be just as difficult for him to climb the tree."

"We have to do something," Violet insisted. "This poem isn't just a couplet—it's a cry for help. Isadora herself says 'Only you can end our fear.' Our friends are frightened, and it's up to us to rescue them."

Hector took some oven mitts out of the pocket of his overalls, and used them to take the enchiladas out of the oven. "I'll tell you what," he said. "It's a nice evening, and our chicken enchiladas are done. We can sit out on the porch, and eat our dinner, and keep an eye on Nevermore Tree. This area is so flat that even at night you can see for quite a distance, and if Count Olaf approaches—or anybody else, for that matter—we'll see him coming."

"But Count Olaf might perform his treachery after dinner," Klaus said. "The only way to make sure that nobody approaches the tree is to watch the tree all night."

"We can take turns sleeping," Violet said, "so that one of us is always awake to keep watch."

Hector started to shake his head, but then stopped and looked at the children. "Normally I don't approve of children staying up late," he said finally, "unless they are reading a very good book, seeing a wonderful movie, or attending a dinner party with fascinating guests. But this time I suppose we can make an exception. I'll probably fall asleep, but you three can keep watch all night if you wish. Just please don't try to climb Nevermore Tree in the dark. I understand how frustrated you are, and I know that the only thing we can do is wait until morning."

The Baudelaires looked at one another and sighed. They were so anxious about the

Quagmires that they wanted to run right out and climb Nevermore Tree, but they knew in their hearts that Hector was right.

"I guess you're right, Hector," Violet said. "We can wait until morning."

"It's the only thing we can do," Klaus agreed.

"Contraire!" Sunny said, and held up her arms so that Klaus could pick her up. She meant something along the lines of "I can think of something else we can do—hold me up to the window latch!" and her brother did so. Sunny's tiny fingers undid the latch of the window and pushed it open, letting in the cool evening air and the muttering sound of the crows. Then she leaned forward as far as she could and stuck her head out into the night. "Bark!" she cried out as loudly as she could. "Bark!"

There are many expressions to describe someone who is going about something in the wrong way. "Making a mistake" is one way to describe this situation. "Screwing up" is another, although it is a bit rude, and "Attempting to rescue Lemony Snicket by writing letters to a congressman, instead of digging an escape tunnel" is a third way, although it is a bit too specific. But Sunny calling out "Bark!" brings to mind an expression that, sadly enough, describes the situation perfectly.

By "Bark!" Sunny meant "If you're up there, Quagmires, just hang on, and we'll get you out first thing in the morning," and I'm sorry to say that the expression which best describes her circumstances is "barking up the wrong tree." It was a kind gesture of Sunny's, to try to reassure Isadora and Duncan that the Baudelaires would help them escape from Count Olaf's clutches, but the youngest Baudelaire was going about it the wrong way. "Bark!" she cried one more time, as Hector began to dish up the chicken enchiladas, and led the Baudelaires to the front porch so they could eat at the picnic table and keep an eye on Nevermore Tree, but Sunny was making a mistake. The Baudelaires did not realize the mistake as they finished their dinner and kept their eye on the immense, muttering tree. They did not realize the mistake as they sat on the porch for the rest of the night, taking turns at squinting at the flat horizon for any sign of someone approaching and dozing beside Hector using the picnic table as a pillow. But when the sun began to rise, and one V.F.D. crow left Nevermore Tree and began to fly in a circle, and three more crows followed, and then seven more, and then twelve more, and soon the morning sky was filled with the sound of fluttering wings as the thousands of crows circled and circled above the children's heads as they rose from the wooden chairs and walked quickly toward the tree to look for any sign of the Quagmires, the Baudelaires saw at once how deeply mistaken they had been.

Without the murder of crows roosting in its branches, Nevermore Tree looked as bare as a skeleton. There was not a single leaf among the hundreds and hundreds of the tree's branches. Standing on its scraggly roots and looking up into the empty branches, the Baudelaires could see every last detail of Nevermore Tree, and they could see at once that they would not find Duncan and Isadora Quagmire no matter how far they climbed. It was an enormous tree, and it was a sturdy tree, and it was apparently very comfortable to roost in, but it was the wrong tree. Klaus had been barking up the wrong tree when he'd said that their kidnapped friends were probably up there, and Violet had been barking up the wrong tree when she'd said that they should climb up and look for them, and Sunny had been barking up the wrong tree when she'd said "Bark!" The Baudelaire orphans had been barking up the wrong tree all evening, because the only thing the children found that morning was another scrap of paper, rolled into a scroll, among all the black feathers that the crows had left behind.

CHAPTER
Five

Until dawn comes we cannot speak.
No words can come from this sad beak.

"My head is spinning again," Violet said, holding the scrap of paper so Klaus and Sunny could see what was written on it. "And my legs are all wobbly and my body is buzzing, like I've been struck by lightning. How in the world did Isadora get another poem here? We made sure that one of us was watching the tree at every moment."

"Maybe it was here yesterday, but Hector didn't see it," Klaus said.

Violet shook her head. "A white scrap of paper is very easy to see next to all these black feathers. It must have arrived here sometime in the night. But how?"

"How it got here is the least of our questions," Klaus said. "Where are the Quagmires? That's the question I want answered."

"But why doesn't Isadora just tell us," Violet said, rereading the couplet and frowning, "instead of leaving us mysterious poems on the ground where anyone could find them?"

"Maybe that's why," Klaus said slowly. "Anyone could find them here on the ground. If Isadora simply wrote out where they were, and Count Olaf found the scrap of paper, he'd move them—or worse. I'm not that experienced with reading poetry, but I bet Isadora *is* telling us where she and her brother are. It must be hidden somewhere in the poem."

"It'll be difficult to find," Violet said, rereading the couplet. "There are so many confusing things about this poem. Why does she say 'beak'? Isadora has a nose and mouth, not a beak."

"Cra!" Sunny said, which meant "She probably means the beak of a V.F.D. crow."

"You might be right," Violet agreed. "But why does she say that no words can come from it? Of course no words can come from a beak. Birds can't talk."

"Actually, some birds can talk," Klaus said. "I read an ornithological encyclopedia that discussed the parrot and the myna bird, which both can imitate human speech."

"But there aren't any parrots or myna birds around here," Violet said. "There are only crows, and crows certainly can't speak."

"And speaking of speaking," Klaus said, "why does the poem say 'Until dawn comes we cannot speak'?"

"Well, both these poems arrived in the morning," Violet said. "Maybe Isadora means that she can only send us poems in the morning."

"None of this makes any sense," Klaus said. "Maybe Hector can help us figure out what's going wrong."

"Laper!" Sunny said in agreement, and the children went to wake up the handyman, who was still asleep on the front porch. Violet touched his shoulder, and as he yawned and sat up the children could see that his face had lines on it from sleeping on the picnic table.

"Good morning, Baudelaires," he said, stretching his arms and giving them a sleepy smile. "At least, I hope it's a good morning. Did you find any sign of the Quagmires?"

"It's more like a strange morning," Violet replied. "We found a sign of them, all right. Take a look."

Violet handed Hector the second poem, and he read it and frowned. "'Curiouser and curiouser,'" he said, quoting one of the Baudelaires' favorite books. "This is really turning into a puzzle."

"But a puzzle is just something you do for amusement," Klaus said. "Duncan and Isadora are in grave danger. If we don't figure out what these poems are trying to tell us, Count Olaf will—"

"Don't even say it," Violet said with a shiver. "We absolutely must solve this puzzle, and that is that."

Hector stood up to stretch, and looked out on the flat and empty horizon surrounding his home. "Judging by the angle of the sun," he said, "it's just about time to leave. We don't even have time for breakfast."

"Leave?" Violet asked.

"Of course," Hector said. "Are you forgetting how many chores we have ahead of us today?" He reached into the pocket of his overalls and pulled out a list. "We begin downtown, of course, so the crows don't get in our way. We have to trim Mrs. Morrow's hedges, wash Mr.

Lesko's windows, and polish all the doorknobs at the Verhoogen family's mansion. Plus we have to sweep all the feathers out of the street, and take out everyone's garbage and recyclables."

"But the Quagmire kidnapping is much more important than any of those things," Violet said.

Hector sighed. "I agree with you," he said, "but I'm not going to argue with the Council of Elders. They make me too skittish."

"I'll be happy to explain the situation to them," Klaus said.

"No," Hector decided. "It will be best to do our chores as usual. Go wash your faces, Baudelaires, and then we'll go."

The Baudelaires looked at one another in dismay, wishing that the handyman wasn't quite so afraid of a group of old people wearing crow-shaped hats, but without further discussion they walked back into the house, washed their faces, and followed Hector across the flat landscape until they reached the outskirts of town and then through the uptown district, where the V.F.D. crows were roosting, until they reached the downtown house of Mrs. Morrow, who was waiting in her pink robe on her front porch. Without a word she handed Hector a pair of hedge clippers, which are nothing more than large scissors designed to cut branches and leaves rather than paper, and gave each Baudelaire a large plastic bag to gather up the leaves and branches Hector would snip off. Hedge clippers and a plastic bag are not appropriate methods of greeting someone, of course, particularly first thing in the morning, but the three siblings were so busy thinking about what the poems could mean that they scarcely noticed. As they gathered up the hedge trimmings they floated several theories— the phrase "floated several theories" here means "talked quietly about the two couplets by Isadora Quagmire"—until the hedge looked nice and neat and it was time to walk down the block to where Mr. Lesko lived. Mr. Lesko— whom the Baudelaires recognized as the man in plaid pants who was worried that the children might have to live with him—was even ruder than Mrs. Morrow. He merely pointed at a pile of window-cleaning supplies and stomped back into his house, but once again the Baudelaires were concentrating on solving the mystery of the two messages they had been left, and scarcely noticed Mr. Lesko's rudeness. Violet and Klaus each began scrubbing dirt off a window with a damp rag, while Sunny stood by with a bucket of soapy water and Hector climbed up to clean the windows on the second floor, but all the children thought of was each line of Isadora's confusing poem, until they were finished with the windows and were ready to go to work on the rest of the chores for the day, which I will not describe for you, not only because they were so boring that I would fall asleep while writing them down on paper, but because the Baudelaire orphans scarcely noticed them. The children thought about the couplets while they polished the Verhoogen doorknobs, and they thought about them when they swept the feathers from the street into a dustpan that Sunny held while crawling in front of her siblings, but they still could not imagine how Isadora managed to leave a poem underneath Nevermore Tree. They thought about the couplets as they carried the garbage and recyclables from all of V.F.D.'s downtown residents, and they thought about them as they ate a lunch of cabbage sandwiches that one of V.F.D.'s restaurant owners had agreed to provide as his part in the village's attempt to raise the children, but they still could not figure out what Isadora was trying to tell them. They thought of the couplets when Hector read out the list of afternoon chores, which included such tedious duties as making citizens' beds, washing townspeople's dishes, preparing enough hot fudge sundaes for the entire Council of Elders to enjoy as an afternoon snack, and polishing Fowl Fountain, but no matter how hard they thought, the Baudelaires got no closer to solving the couplets' mysteries.

"I'm very impressed with how hard you three children are working," Hector said, as he and the children began their last afternoon chore. Fowl Fountain was made in the shape of an enormous crow, and stood in the middle of the uptown district, in a courtyard with many different streets leading out of it. The children were scrubbing at the crow's metal body, which was covered in carvings of feather shapes to make it look more realistic. Hector was standing on a ladder scrubbing at the crow's metal head, which was facing straight up and spitting a steady stream of water out of a hole fashioned to look like its mouth, as if the enormous bird were gargling and spitting water all over its own body. The effect was hideous, but the V.F.D. crows must have thought differently, because the fountain was covered in feathers that they had left behind during their uptown morning roost. "When the Council of Elders told me that the village was serving as your guardian,"

Hector continued, "I was afraid that three small children wouldn't be able to do all these chores without complaining."

"We're used to strenuous exercise," Violet replied. "When we lived in Paltryville, we debarked trees and sawed them into boards, and at Prufrock Preparatory School we had to run hundreds of laps every night."

"Besides," Klaus said, "we're so busy thinking about the couplets that we've scarcely noticed our work."

"I thought that's why you were so quiet," Hector said. "How do the poems go again?"

The Baudelaires had looked at the two scraps of paper so many times over the course of the day that they could recite both poems from memory.

> *"For sapphires we are held in here.*
> *Only you can end our fear."*

Violet said.

"Until dawn comes we cannot speak.
No words can come from this sad beak."

Klaus said.

"Dulch!" Sunny added, which meant something like, "And we still haven't figured out what they really mean."

"They're tricky, all right," Hector said. "In fact, I . . ."

Here his voice trailed off, and the children were startled to see the handyman turn around so he was no longer facing them and begin to scrub the left eye of the metal crow, as if someone had flicked a switch that stopped him from talking.

"Fowl Fountain still doesn't look completely clean," said a stern voice from behind the children, and the Baudelaires turned around to see three women from the Council of Elders who had entered the courtyard and now stood frowning at them. Hector was so skittish that he didn't even look up to answer, but the children were not nearly as intimidated, a word which here means "made skittish by three older women wearing crow-shaped hats."

"We're not completely finished cleaning it," Violet explained politely. "I do hope you enjoyed your hot fudge sundaes that we prepared for you earlier."

"They were O.K.," one of them said, with a shrug that bobbed her crow hat slightly.

"Mine had too many nuts," another one of them said. "Rule #961 clearly states that the Council of Elders' hot fudge sundaes cannot have more than fifteen pieces of nuts each, and mine might have had more than that."

"I'm very sorry to hear that," Klaus said, not adding that anyone who is so picky about a hot fudge sundae should make it themselves.

"We've stacked up the dirty ice cream dishes in the Snack Hut," the third one said. "Tomorrow afternoon you'll wash them as part of your uptown chores. But we came to tell Hector something."

The children looked up to the top of the ladder, thinking that Hector would have to turn around and speak to them now, no matter how skittish he was. But he merely gave a little cough, and continued to scrub at Fowl Fountain. Violet remembered what her father had taught her to say when he was unable to come to the phone, and she spoke up.

"I'm sorry," she said. "Hector is occupied at the moment. May I give him a message?"

The Elders looked at one another and nodded, which made it look like their hats were pecking at one another. "I suppose so," one of them said. "If we can trust a little girl like you to deliver it."

"The message is very important," the second one said, and once again I find it necessary to use the expression "bolt from the blue." You would think, after the mysterious appearance of not one but two poems by Isadora Quagmire at the base of Nevermore Tree, that no more bolts from the blue would appear in the village of V.F.D. A bolt of lightning, after all, rarely comes down from a clear blue sky and strikes the exact same place more than once. But for the Baudelaire orphans, life seemed to be little else than bolt after unfortunate bolt from the blue, ever since Mr. Poe had delivered the first bolt from the blue in telling them that their parents had been killed, and no matter how many bolts from the blue they experienced, their heads never spun any less, and their legs never got less wobbly, and their bodies never buzzed any less with astonishment when another bolt arrived from the blue. So when the Baudelaires heard the Elders' message, they almost had to sit down in Fowl Fountain, because the message was such an utter surprise. It was a message that they thought they might never hear, and it is a message that only reaches me in my most pleasant dreams, which are few and far between.

"The message is this," said the third member of the Council of Elders, and she leaned her head in close so that the children could see every felt feather of her crow hat. "Count Olaf has been captured," she said, and the Baudelaires felt as if a bolt of lightning had struck them once more.

CHAPTER Six

Although "jumping to conclusions" is an expression, rather than an activity, it is as dangerous as jumping off a cliff, jumping in front of a moving train, and jumping for joy. If you jump off a cliff, you have a very good chance of experiencing a painful landing unless there is something below you to cushion your fall, such as a body of water or an immense pile of tissue paper. If you jump in front of a moving train, you have a very good chance of experiencing a painful voyage unless you are wearing some sort of train-proof suit. And if you jump for joy, you have a very good chance of experiencing a painful bump on the head, unless you make sure you are standing some-place with very high ceilings, which joyous people rarely do. Clearly, the solution to any-thing involving jumping is either to make sure you are jumping to a safe place, or not to jump at all.

But it is hard not to jump at all when you are jumping to conclusions, and it is impossible to make sure that you are jumping to a safe place, because all "jumping to conclusions" means is that you are believing something is true even though you don't actually know whether it is or not. When the Baudelaire orphans heard from the three members of V.F.D.'s Council of Elders that Count Olaf had been captured, they were so excited that they immediately jumped to the conclusion that it was true.

"It's true," said one of the Elders, which didn't help things any. "A man arrived in town this morning, with one eyebrow and a tattoo of an eye on his ankle."

"It must be Olaf," Violet said, jumping to conclusions.

"Of course it is," the second Council member said. "He matched the description that Mr. Poe gave us, so we arrested him immediately."

"So it's true," Klaus said, joining his sister in the jump. "You've really captured Count Olaf."

"Of course it's true," the third woman said impatiently. "We've even contacted *The Daily Punctilio*, and they'll write a story about it. Soon the whole world will know that Count Olaf has been captured at last."

"Hooray!" cried Sunny, the last Baudelaire to jump to conclusions.

"The Council of Elders has called a special meeting," said the woman who appeared to be the eldest Elder. Her crow hat bobbed in excitement as she spoke. "All citizens are required to go to Town Hall immediately, to discuss what is to be done with him. After all, Rule #19,833 clearly states that no villains are allowed within the city limits. The usual punishment for breaking a rule is burning at the stake."

"Burning at the stake?" Violet said.

"Of course," an Elder said. "Whenever we capture rulebreakers, we tie them to a wooden pole and light a fire underneath their feet. That's why I warned you about the number of nuts on my hot fudge sundae. It would be a shame to light you on fire."

"You mean the punishment is the same, no matter what rule you break?" Klaus asked.

"Of course," another Elder replied. "Rule #2 clearly states that anyone who breaks a rule is burned at the stake. If we didn't burn a rule-breaker at the stake, we would be rulebreakers ourselves, and someone else would have to burn us at the stake. Understand?"

"Sort of," Violet said, although in truth she

didn't understand it at all. None of the Baudelaires did. Although they despised Count Olaf,
the children didn't like the idea of lighting him
on fire. Burning a villain at the stake felt like
something a villain would do rather than something done by fowl devotees.

"But Count Olaf isn't just a rulebreaker,"
Klaus said, choosing his words very carefully.
"He has committed all sorts of terrible crimes. It
would seem best to turn him over to the authorities, rather than burning him at the stake."

"Well, that's something we can talk about at
the meeting," a Councilwoman said, "and we'd
better hurry or we'll be late. Hector, get down
from that ladder."

Hector didn't answer, but he got down from
the ladder and followed the three members of
the Council of Elders away from Fowl Fountain,
keeping his eyes on the ground at all times. The
Baudelaires followed Hector, their stomachs
fluttering as they walked through the uptown
district to the downtown one, where the crows

were roosting as they had been yesterday, when the children had first arrived in V.F.D. Their stomachs were fluttering with relief and excitement, because they believed that Count Olaf had been captured, but also with nervousness and fear, because they hated the idea that he might be burned at the stake. The punishment for V.F.D. rulebreakers made the Baudelaires remember their parents' deaths, and they didn't like the idea of anyone being lit on fire, no matter how vile a person they were. It was unpleasant to feel relief, excitement, nervousness, and fear all at once, and by the time they arrived at Town Hall, the stomachs of the Baudelaire orphans were as fluttery as the crows, which were muttering and scuffling as far as the eye could see.

When one's stomach is as fluttery as all that, it is nice to take a short break to lie down and perhaps sip a fizzy beverage, but there was no time for such things. The three members of the

Council led the way to the large room in Town Hall decorated with portraits of crows. The room was in pandemonium, a phrase which here means "filled with Elders and townspeople standing around arguing." The Baudelaires scanned the room for a sign of Olaf, but it was impossible to see anyone over the bobbing crow heads.

"We need to begin the meeting!" called one of the Council. "Elders, find your places on the bench. Townspeople, find your places on folding chairs." The townspeople stopped talking at once and hurried into their seats, perhaps afraid that they would be burned at the stake if they didn't sit down quickly enough. Violet and Klaus sat down next to Hector, who was still staring at the floor in silence, and picked up Sunny so she could see.

"Hector, place Officer Luciana and Count Olaf on the platform for discussion," an Elder ordered, as the last few townspeople sat down.

"There's no need," called out a grand voice from the back of the room, and the children turned around to see Officer Luciana, with a big red grin beneath the visor of her helmet. "I can get to the platform myself. After all, I'm the Chief of Police."

"That's true," another Elder said, and several other people on the bench nodded their crow hats in agreement as Luciana strolled to the platform, each of her black boots making a loud *clunk!* on the shiny floor.

"I'm proud to say," Officer Luciana said proudly, "that I've already made the first arrest of my career as Chief of Police. Isn't that smashing?"

"Hear, hear!" cried several townspeople.

"And now," Luciana continued, "let's meet the man we're all dying to burn at the stake—Count Olaf!"

With a grand gesture, Officer Luciana stepped off the platform, clunked to the back of the room, and dragged a frightened-looking man out of a folding chair. He was dressed in a rumpled suit with a large rip across the shoulder, and a pair of shiny silver handcuffs. He wasn't wearing any shoes or socks, and as Officer Luciana marched him to the platform the children could see that he had a tattoo of an eye on his left ankle, just like Count Olaf had. And when he turned his head and gazed around the room, the children could see that he had only one eyebrow, instead of two, just like Count Olaf had. But the children could also see that he wasn't Count Olaf. He wasn't as tall as Count Olaf, and he wasn't quite as thin, and there wasn't dirt under his fingernails, or a nasty and greedy look in his eyes. But most of all the Baudelaires could see that he wasn't Count Olaf the way you could tell that a stranger wasn't your uncle, even if he were wearing the same polka-dot coat and curly wig that your uncle always wore. The three siblings looked at one another, and then at the man being dragged onto the platform, and they realized with a sinking feeling that they had been jumping to conclusions about Olaf's capture.

"Ladies and gentlemen," Officer Luciana said, "and orphans, I give you Count Olaf!"

"But I'm not Count Olaf!" the man cried. "My name is Jacques, and—"

"Silence!" commanded one of the meanest-looking members of the Council of Elders. "Rule #920 clearly states that no one may talk while on the platform."

"Let's burn him at the stake!" cried a voice, and the children turned to see Mr. Lesko standing up and pointing at the trembling man on the platform. "We haven't burned anyone at the stake for a long time!"

Several members of the Council nodded their heads. "That's a good point," one of them said.

"He's Olaf, all right," Mrs. Morrow called from the far side of the room. "He has one eyebrow instead of two, and there's a tattoo of an eye on his ankle."

"But lots of people have only one eyebrow,"

Jacques cried, "and I have this tattoo as part of my job."

"And your job is villain!" Mr. Lesko called out triumphantly. "Rule #19,833 clearly states that no villains are allowed within the city limits, so we get to burn you at the stake!"

"Hear, hear!" called several voices in agreement.

"I'm not a villain!" Jacques said frantically. "I work for the volunteer—"

"Enough is enough!" said one of the youngest Elders. "Olaf, you have already been warned about Rule #920. You are not allowed to speak when you are on the platform. Do any more citizens wish to speak before we schedule the burning of Olaf at the stake?"

Violet stood up, which is not an easy thing to do if your head is still spinning, your legs are still wobbly, and your body is still buzzing with astonishment. "I wish to speak," she said. "The town of V.F.D. is my guardian, and so I am a citizen."

Klaus, who had Sunny in his arms, stood up and took his place beside his sister. "This man," he said, pointing at Jacques, "is not Count Olaf. Officer Luciana has made a mistake in arresting him, and we don't want to make things worse by burning an innocent man at the stake."

Jacques gave the children a grateful smile, but Officer Luciana turned around and clunked over to where the Baudelaires were standing. The children could not see her eyes, because the visor on her helmet was still down, but her bright red lips curled into a tight smile. "It is you who are making things worse," she said, and then turned to the Council of Elders. "Obviously, the shock of seeing Count Olaf has confused these children," she said to them.

"Of course it has!" agreed an Elder. "Speaking as a member of the town serving as their legal guardian, I say that these children clearly need to be put to bed. Now, are there any adults who wish to speak?"

The Baudelaires looked over at Hector, in

the hopes that he would overcome his nervousness and stand up to speak. Surely he didn't
believe that the three siblings were so confused
that they didn't know who Count Olaf was. But
Hector did not rise to the occasion, a phrase
which here means "continued to sit in his folding chair with his eyes cast downward," and
after a moment the Council of Elders closed the
matter.

"I hereby close the matter," an Elder said.
"Hector, please take the Baudelaires home."

"Yes!" called out a member of the Verhoogen
family. "Put the orphans to bed and burn Olaf
at the stake!"

"Hear, hear!" several voices cried.

One of the Council of Elders shook his
head. "It's too late to burn anyone at the stake
today," he said, and there was a mutter of disappointment from the townspeople. "We will
burn Count Olaf at the stake right after breakfast," he continued. "All uptown residents
should bring flaming torches, and all downtown

residents should bring wood for kindling and some sort of healthy snack. See you tomorrow."

"And in the meantime," Officer Luciana announced, "I will keep him in the uptown jail, across from Fowl Fountain."

"But I'm innocent!" the man on the platform cried. "Please listen to me, I beg of you! I'm not Count Olaf! My name is Jacques!" He turned to the three siblings, who could see he had tears in his eyes. "Oh, Baudelaires," he said, "I am so relieved to see that you are alive. Your parents—"

"That's enough out of you," Officer Luciana said, clasping her white-gloved hand over Jacques's mouth.

"Pipit!" Sunny shrieked, which meant "Wait!" but Officer Luciana either didn't listen or didn't care, and she quickly dragged Jacques out the door before he could say another word. The townspeople rose up in their folding chairs to watch him go, and then began talking among themselves as the Council of Elders left the bench. The Baudelaires saw Mr. Lesko share a joke with the Verhoogen family, as if the entire evening had been a jolly party instead of a meeting sentencing an innocent man to death. "Pipit!" Sunny shrieked again, but nobody listened. His eyes still on the floor, Hector took Violet and Klaus by the hand and led them out of Town Hall. The handyman did not say a word, and the Baudelaires didn't, either. Their stomachs felt too fluttery and their hearts too heavy to even open their mouths. As they left the council meeting without another glimpse of Jacques or Officer Luciana, they felt a pain even worse than that of jumping to conclusions. The children felt as if they had jumped off a cliff, or jumped in front of a moving train. As they stepped out of Town Hall into the still night air, the Baudelaire orphans felt as if they would never jump for joy again.

In this large and fierce world of ours, there are many, many unpleasant places to be. You can be in a river swarming with angry electric eels, or in a supermarket filled with vicious long-distance runners. You can be in a hotel that has no room service, or you can be lost in a forest that is slowly filling up with water. You can be in a hornet's nest or in an abandoned airport or in the office of a pediatric surgeon, but one of the most unpleasant things that can happen is to find yourself in a quandary, which is where the Baudelaire orphans found themselves that night. Finding yourself in a quandary means that everything seems confusing and dangerous and you don't know what in the world to do about it, and it is one of the worst unpleasantries you can encounter. The three Baudelaires sat in Hector's kitchen as the handyman prepared another Mexican dinner, and compared with the quandary they were in, all their other problems felt like the small potatoes he was chopping into thirds.

"Everything seems confusing," Violet said glumly. "The Quagmire triplets are somewhere nearby, but we don't know where, and the only clues we have are two confusing poems. And now, there's a man who isn't Count Olaf, but he has an eye tattooed on his ankle, and he wanted to tell us something about our parents."

"It's more than confusing," Klaus said. "It's dangerous. We need to rescue the Quagmires before Count Olaf does something dreadful, and we need to convince the Council of Elders that the man they arrested is really Jacques, other-wise they'll burn him at the stake."

"Quandary?" Sunny said, which meant something along the lines of "What in the world can we do about it?"

"I don't know what we *can* do about it, Sunny," Violet replied. "We spent all day trying to figure out what the poems meant, and we tried our best to convince the Council of Elders that Officer Luciana made a mistake." She and her siblings looked at Hector, who had certainly not tried his best with the Council of Elders but instead had sat in his folding chair without saying a word.

Hector sighed and looked unhappily at the children. "I know I should have said some-thing," he told them, "but I was far too skittish. The Council of Elders is so imposing that I can never say a word in their presence. However, I can think of something that we can do to help."

"What is it?" Klaus asked.

"We can enjoy these huevos rancheros," he

said. "Huevos rancheros are fried eggs and beans, served with tortillas and potatoes in a spicy tomato sauce."

The siblings looked at one another, trying to imagine how a Mexican dish would get them out of their quandary. "How will that help?" Violet asked doubtfully.

"I don't know," Hector admitted. "But they're almost ready, and my recipe is a delicious one, if I do say so myself. Come on, let's eat. Maybe a good dinner will help you think of something."

The children sighed, but nodded their heads in agreement and got up to set the table, and curiously enough, a good dinner did in fact help the Baudelaires think of something. As Violet took her first bite of beans, she felt the gears and levers of her inventing brain spring into action. As Klaus dipped his tortilla into the spicy tomato sauce, he began to think of books he had read that might be helpful. And as Sunny smeared egg yolks all over her face, she clicked her four sharp teeth together and tried to think of a way that they might be useful. By the time the Baudelaires were finishing the meal Hector had prepared for them, their ideas had grown and developed into full-fledged plans, just as Nevermore Tree had grown a long time ago from a tiny seed and Fowl Fountain had been built recently from someone's hideous blueprint.

It was Sunny who spoke up first. "Plan!" she said.

"What is it, Sunny?" Klaus asked.

With a tiny finger covered in tomato sauce, Sunny pointed out the window at Nevermore Tree, which was covered in the V.F.D. crows as it was every evening. "Merganser!" she said firmly.

"My sister says that tomorrow morning there will probably be another poem from Isadora in the same spot," Klaus explained to Hector. "She wants to spend the night underneath the tree. She's so small that whoever is delivering the poems probably won't spot her, and she'll be able to find out how the couplets are getting to us."

"And that should bring us closer to finding the Quagmires," Violet said. "That's a good plan, Sunny."

"My goodness, Sunny," Hector said. "Won't you be frightened spending all night underneath a whole murder of crows?"

"Therill," Sunny said, which meant "It won't be any more frightening than the time I climbed up an elevator shaft with my teeth."

"I think I have a good plan, too," Klaus said. "Hector, yesterday you told us about the secret library you have in the barn."

"Ssh!" Hector said, looking around the kitchen. "Not so loud! You know it's against the rules to have all those books, and I don't want to be burned at the stake."

"I don't want *anyone* to be burned at the stake," Klaus said. "Now, does the secret library contain books about the rules of V.F.D.?"

"Absolutely," Hector said. "Lots of them.

Because the rule books describe people breaking the rules, they break Rule #108, which clearly states that the V.F.D. library cannot contain any books that break any of the rules."

"Well, I'm going to read as many rule books as I can," Klaus said. "There must be a way to save Jacques from being burned at the stake, and I bet I'll find it in the pages of those books."

"My word, Klaus," Hector said. "Won't you be bored reading all those rule books?"

"It won't be any more boring than the time I had to read all about grammar, in order to save Aunt Josephine," he replied.

"Sunny is working to save the Quagmires," Violet said, "and Klaus is working to save Jacques. I've got to work to save *us*."

"What do you mean?" Klaus asked.

"Well, I think Count Olaf must be behind all this trouble," Violet said.

"Grebe!" Sunny said, which meant "As usual!"

"If the town of V.F.D. burns Jacques at the

stake," Violet continued, "then everyone will think Count Olaf is dead. I bet *The Daily Punctilio* will even have a story that says so. It will be very good news for Olaf—the real one, that is. If everyone thinks he's dead, Olaf can be as treacherous as he likes, and the authorities won't come looking for him."

"That's true," Klaus said. "Count Olaf must have found Jacques—whoever he is—and brought him into town. He knew that Officer Luciana would think he was Olaf. But what does that have to do with saving us?"

"Well, if we rescue the Quagmires and prove that Jacques is innocent," Violet said, "Count Olaf will come after us, and we can't rely on the Council of Elders to protect us."

"Poe!" Sunny said.

"Or Mr. Poe," Violet agreed. "That's why we'll need a way to save ourselves." She turned to Hector. "Yesterday, you also told us about your self-sustaining hot air mobile home."

Hector looked around the kitchen again, to

make sure no one was listening. "Yes," he said, "but I think I'm going to stop work on it. If the Council of Elders learns that I'm breaking Rule #67, I could be burned at the stake. Anyway, I can't seem to get the engine to work."

"If you don't mind, I'd like to take a look at it," Violet said. "Maybe I could help finish it. You wanted to use the self-sustaining hot air mobile home to escape from V.F.D. and the Council of Elders and everything else that makes you skittish, but it would also make an excellent escape vehicle."

"Maybe it could be both," Hector said shyly, and reached across the table to pat Sunny on the shoulder. "I very much enjoy the company of you three children, and it would be delightful to share a mobile home with you. There's plenty of room in the self-sustaining hot air mobile home, and once we get it to work we could launch it and never come down. Count Olaf and his associates would never be able to bother you again. What do you think?"

The three Baudelaires listened closely to Hector's suggestion, but when they tried to tell him what they thought, it felt like they were in a quandary all over again. On one hand, it would be exciting to live in such an unusual way, and the thought of being safe forever from Count Olaf's evil clutches was very appealing, to say the least. Violet looked at her baby sister and thought about the promise she had made, when Sunny was born, that she would always look after her younger siblings and make sure they wouldn't get into trouble. Klaus looked at Hector, who was the only citizen in this vile village who really seemed to care about the children, as a guardian should. And Sunny looked out the window at the evening sky, and remembered the first time she and her siblings saw the V.F.D. crows fly in superlative circles and wished that they, too, could escape from all their worries. But on the other hand, the Baudelaires felt that flying away from all their trouble, and living forever up in the sky, didn't seem to be a proper way to live one's life. Sunny was a baby, Klaus was only twelve, and even Violet, the eldest, was fourteen, which is not really so old. The Baudelaires had many things they hoped to accomplish on the ground, and they weren't sure that they could simply abandon all those hopes so early in their lives. The Baudelaires sat at the table and thought about Hector's plan, and it seemed to the children that if they spent the rest of their lives floating around the heavens, they simply wouldn't be in their element, a phrase which here means "in the sort of home the three siblings would prefer."

"First things first," Violet said finally, hoping that she wasn't hurting Hector's feelings. "Before we make a decision about the rest of our lives, let's get Duncan and Isadora out of Olaf's clutches."

"And make sure Jacques won't be burned at the stake," Klaus said.

"Albico!" Sunny added, which meant something like, "And let's solve the mystery of V.F.D.

that the Quagmires told us about!"

Hector sighed. "You're right," he said. "Those things are more important, even if they do make me skittish. Well, let's take Sunny to the tree and then it's off to the barn, where the library and inventing studio are. It looks like it's going to be another long night, but hopefully this time we won't be barking up the wrong tree."

The Baudelaires smiled at the handyman and followed him out into the night, which was cool and breezy and filled with the sounds of the murder of crows settling down for the night. They kept on smiling as they separated, with Sunny crawling toward Nevermore Tree and the two older Baudelaires following Hector to the barn, and they continued to smile as they began to put each of their plans into action. Violet smiled because Hector's inventing studio was very well-equipped, with plenty of pliers and glue and wire and everything her inventing brain needed, and because Hector's self-sustaining hot air mobile home was an enormous, fascinating mechanism—just the sort of challenging invention she loved to work on. Klaus smiled because Hector's library was very comfortable, with some good sturdy tables and cushioned chairs just perfect for reading in, and because the books on the rules of V.F.D. were very thick and full of difficult words—just the sort of challenging reading he enjoyed. And Sunny smiled because there were several dead branches of Nevermore Tree that had fallen to the ground, so she would have something to gnaw on as she hid and waited for the next couplet to arrive. The children were in their elements. Violet was in her element at the inventing studio, and Klaus was in his element at the library, and Sunny was in hers just from being low to the ground and near something she could bite. Violet tied her hair up in a ribbon to keep it out of her eyes, and Klaus polished his glasses, and Sunny stretched her mouth to get her teeth ready for the task ahead of her, and the three siblings smiled more than

they had since their arrival in town. The Baudelaire orphans were in their elements, and they
hoped that being in their elements would lead
them out of their quandary.

The next morning began with a colorful and lengthy sunrise, which Sunny saw from her hiding place at the bottom of Nevermore Tree. It continued with the sounds of awakening crows, which Klaus heard from the library in the barn, and followed with the sight of the birds making their familiar circle in the sky, which Violet saw just as she was leaving the inventing studio. By the time Klaus joined his sister outside the barn, and Sunny crawled across the flat landscape to reach them, the birds had stopped circling and were flying together uptown, and the morning was so pretty and peaceful that as

I describe it I can almost forget that it was a very, very sad morning for me, a morning that I wish I could strike forever from the Snicket calendar. But I can't erase this day, any more than I can write a happy ending to this book, for the simple reason that the story does not go that way. No matter how lovely the morning was, or how confident the Baudelaires felt about what they had discovered over the course of the night, there isn't a happy ending on the horizon of this story, any more than there was an elephant on the horizon of V.F.D.

"Good morning," Violet said to Klaus, and yawned.

"Good morning," Klaus replied. He was holding two books in his arms, but nevertheless he managed to wave at Sunny, who was still crawling toward them. "How did everything go with Hector in the inventing studio?"

"Well, Hector fell asleep a few hours ago," Violet said, "but I discovered a few small flaws in the self-sustaining hot air mobile home. The engine conductivity was low, due to some problems with the electromagnetic generator Hector built. This meant that the inflation rate of the balloons was often uneven, so I reconfigured some key conduits. Also, the water circulation system was run on ill-fitting pipes, which meant that the self-sustaining aspect of the food center probably wouldn't last as long as it should, so I rerouted some of the aquacycling."

"Ning!" Sunny called, as she reached her siblings.

"Good morning, Sunny," Klaus said. "Violet was just telling me that she noticed a few things wrong with Hector's invention, but she thinks she fixed them."

"Well, I'd like to test the whole device out before we go up in it, if there's time," Violet said, picking up Sunny and holding her, "but I think everything should work pretty well. It's a fantastic invention. A small group of people could really spend the rest of their lives safely in the air. Did you discover anything in the library?"

"Well, first I discovered that books about V.F.D. rules are actually quite fascinating," Klaus said. "Rule #19, for instance, clearly states that the only pens that are acceptable within the city limits are ones made from the feathers of crows. And yet Rule #39 clearly states that it is illegal to make anything out of crow feathers. How can the townspeople obey both rules at once?"

"Maybe they don't have any pens at all," Violet said, "but that's not important. Did you discover anything helpful in the rule books?"

"Yes," Klaus said, and opened one of the books he was carrying. "Listen to this: Rule #2,493 clearly states that any person who is going to be burned at the stake has the opportunity to make a speech right before the fire is lit. We can go to the uptown jail this morning and make sure Jacques gets that opportunity. In his speech, he can tell people who he really is, and why he has that tattoo."

"But he tried to do that yesterday at the meeting," Violet said. "Nobody believed him. Nobody even *listened* to him."

"I was thinking the same thing," Klaus said, opening the second book, "until I read this."

"Towhee?" Sunny asked, which meant something like "Is there a rule that clearly states that people must listen to speeches?"

"No," Klaus replied. "This isn't a rule book. This is a book about psychology, the study of the mind. It was removed from the library because there's a chapter about the Cherokee tribe of North America. They make all sorts of things out of feathers, which breaks Rule #39."

"That's ridiculous," Violet said.

"I agree," Klaus said, "but I'm glad this book was here, instead of in town, because it gave me an idea. There's a chapter here about mob psychology."

"Wazay?" Sunny asked.

"A mob is a crowd of people," Klaus explained, "usually an angry one."

"Like the townspeople and the Council of Elders yesterday," Violet said, "in Town Hall. They were incredibly angry."

"Exactly," Klaus said. "Now listen to this." The middle Baudelaire opened the second book and began to read out loud. "'The subliminal emotional tenor of a mob's unruliness lies in solitary opinions, expressed emphatically at various points in the stereo field.'"

"Tenor? Stereo?" Violet asked. "It sounds like you're talking about opera."

"The book uses a lot of complicated words," Klaus said, "but luckily there was a dictionary in Hector's library. It had been removed from V.F.D. because it defined the phrase 'mechanical device.' All that sentence means is that if a few people, scattered throughout the crowd, begin to shout their opinions, soon the whole mob will agree with them. It happened in the council meeting yesterday—a few people said angry things, and soon the whole room was angry."

"Vue," Sunny said, which meant "Yes, I remember."

"When we get to the jail," Klaus said, "we'll make sure that Jacques is allowed to give his speech. Then, as he explains himself, we'll scatter ourselves throughout the crowd and shout things like, 'I believe him!' and 'Hear, hear!' Mob psychology should make everyone demand Jacques's freedom."

"Do you really think that will work?" Violet asked.

"Well, I'd prefer to test it first," Klaus said, "just like you'd prefer to test the self-sustaining hot air mobile home. But we don't have time. Now, Sunny, what did you discover from spending the night under a tree?"

Sunny held up one of her small hands to show them another scrap of paper. "Couplet!"

she cried out triumphantly, and her siblings gathered around to read it.

The first thing you read contains the clue:
An initial way to speak to you.

"Good work, Sunny," Violet said. "This is definitely another poem by Isadora Quagmire."

"And it seems to lead us back to the first poem," Klaus said. "It says 'The first thing you read contains the clue.'"

"But what does 'An initial way to speak to you' mean?" Violet asked. "Initials, like V.F.D.?"

"Maybe," Klaus replied, "but the word 'initial' can also mean 'first.' I think Isadora means that this is the first way she can speak to us—through these poems."

"But we already know that," Violet said. "The Quagmires wouldn't have to tell us. Let's look at all the poems together. Maybe it will give us a complete picture."

Violet took the other two poems out of her pocket, and the three children looked at them together.

> *For sapphires we are held in here.*
> *Only you can end our fear.*

> *Until dawn comes we cannot speak.*
> *No words can come from this sad beak.*

> *The first thing you read contains the clue:*
> *An initial way to speak to you.*

"The part about the beak is still the most confusing," Klaus said.

"Leucophrys!" Sunny said, which meant "I think I can explain that—the crows are delivering the couplets."

"How can that be possible?" Violet asked.

"Loidya!" Sunny answered. She meant something like "I'm absolutely sure that nobody approached the tree all night, and at dawn the note dropped down from the branches of the tree."

"I've heard of carrier pigeons," Klaus said. "Those are birds that carry messages for a living. But I've never heard of carrier crows."

"Maybe they don't know that they're carrier crows," Violet said. "The Quagmires could be attaching the scraps of paper to the crows in some way—putting them in their beaks, or in their feathers—and then the poems come loose when they sleep in Nevermore Tree. The triplets must be somewhere in town. But where?"

"Ko!" Sunny cried, pointing to the poems.

"Sunny's right," Klaus said excitedly. "It says 'Until dawn comes we cannot speak.' That means they're attaching the poems in the morning, when the crows roost uptown."

"Well, that's one more reason to get uptown," Violet replied. "We can save Jacques before he's burned at the stake, and search for the Quagmires. Without you, Sunny, we wouldn't know where to look for the Quagmires."

"Hasserin," Sunny said, which meant "And without you, Klaus, we wouldn't know how to save Jacques."

"And without you, Violet," Klaus said, "we'd have no chance of escaping from this town."

"And if we keep standing here," Violet said, "we won't save anybody. Let's go wake up Hector, and get moving. The Council of Elders said they'd burn Jacques at the stake right after breakfast."

"Yikes!" Sunny said, which meant "That doesn't give us much time," so the Baudelaires didn't take much time walking into the barn and through Hector's library, which was so massive that the two Baudelaire sisters could not believe Klaus had managed to find helpful information among the shelves and shelves of books. There were bookshelves so tall you had to stand on a ladder to reach their highest shelves, and ones so short that you had to crawl on the floor to read their titles. There were books that looked too heavy to move, and books that looked too light to stay in one place, and there were books that looked so dull that the sisters could not imagine anyone reading them—but these were the books that were still stacked in huge heaps, spread out on the tables after Klaus's all-night reading session. Violet and Sunny wanted to pause for a moment and take it all in, but they knew that they didn't have much time.

Behind the last bookshelf of the library was Hector's inventing studio, where Klaus and Sunny got their first glimpse of the self-sustaining hot air mobile home, which was a marvelous contraption. Twelve enormous baskets, each about the size of a small room, were stacked up in the corner, connected by all sorts of different tubes, pipes, and wires, and circled around the baskets were a series of large metal tanks, wooden grates, glass jugs, paper bags, plastic containers, and rolls of twine, along with a number of large mechanical devices with buttons, switches, and gears, and a big pile of deflated balloons. The self-sustaining hot air mobile home was so immense and complicated that it reminded the two younger Baudelaires of what they thought of when they pictured Violet's inventive brain, and every piece of it looked so interesting that Klaus and Sunny could scarcely decide what to look at first. But the Baudelaires knew that they didn't have much time, so rather than explain the invention to her siblings, Violet walked quickly over to one of the baskets, which Klaus and Sunny were surprised to see contained a bed, which in turn contained a sleeping Hector.

"Good morning," the handyman said, when Violet gently shook him awake.

"It *is* a good morning," she replied. "We've discovered some marvelous things. We'll explain everything on our way uptown."

"Uptown?" Hector said, stepping out of the basket. "But the crows are roosting uptown. We do the downtown chores in the morning, remember?"

"We're not doing any chores this morning,"

Klaus said firmly. "That's one of the things we need to explain."

Hector yawned, stretched and rubbed his eyes, and then smiled at the three children. "Well, fire away," he said, using a phrase which here means "begin telling me about your plans."

The siblings led Hector back through his inventing studio and secret library and waited while he locked up the barn. Then, as they took their first few steps across the flat landscape toward the uptown district, the Baudelaire orphans fired away. Violet told Hector about the improvements she had made on his invention, and Klaus told him about what he had learned in Hector's library, and Sunny told him—with some translation help from her siblings—about her discovery of how Isadora's poems were being delivered. By the time the Baudelaires were unrolling the last scrap of paper and showing Hector the third couplet, they had already reached the crow-covered outskirts of V.F.D.'s uptown district.

"So the Quagmires are somewhere in the uptown district," Hector said. "But where?"

"I don't know," Violet admitted, "but we'd better try to save Jacques first. Which way is the uptown jail?" Violet asked Hector.

"It's across from Fowl Fountain," the handyman replied, "but it looks like we won't need directions. Look what's ahead of us."

The children looked, and could see some of the townspeople holding flaming torches and walking about a block ahead of them. "It must be after breakfast," Klaus said. "Let's hurry."

The Baudelaires walked as quickly as they could between the muttering crows roosting on the ground, with Hector trailing skittishly behind them, and soon they rounded a corner and reached Fowl Fountain—or at least what they could see of it. The fountain was swarming with crows who were fluttering their wings in the water in order to give themselves a morning bath, and the Baudelaires could scarcely see one metal feather of the hideous landmark. Across the courtyard was a building with bars on the windows and crows on the bars, and the torch-carrying citizens were standing in a half circle around the door of the building. More of V.F.D.'s citizens were arriving from every direction, and the three children could see a few crow-hatted members of the Council of Elders, standing together and listening to something Mrs. Morrow was saying.

"It seems we arrived in the nick of time," Violet said. "We'd better scatter ourselves throughout the crowd. Sunny, you move to the far left. I'll take the far right."

"Roger!" Sunny said, and began crawling her way through the half circle of people.

"I think I'll just stay here," Hector said quietly, looking down at the ground, but the children had no time to argue with him. Klaus began to walk straight down the middle of the crowd.

"Wait!" Klaus called, moving with difficulty

through the people. "Rule #2,493 clearly states that any person who is going to be burned at the stake has the opportunity to make a speech right before the fire is lit!"

"Yes!" Violet cried, from the right-hand side of the crowd. "Let Jacques be heard!"

Officer Luciana stepped right in front of Violet, who almost bumped her head on the Chief's shiny helmet. Beneath the visor of the helmet Violet could see Luciana's lipsticked mouth rise in a very small smile. "It's too late for that," she said, and a few townspeople around her murmured in agreement. With a *clunk!* of one boot, she stepped aside and let Violet see what had happened. From the left-hand side of the crowd, Sunny crawled over the shoes of the person standing closest to the jail, and Klaus peered over Mr. Lesko's shoulder to get a good look at what everyone was staring at.

Jacques was lying on the ground with his eyes closed, and two members of the Council of Elders were pulling a white sheet over him, as if they were tucking him in for a nap. But as dearly as I wish I could write that it was so, he was not sleeping. The Baudelaires had reached the uptown jail before the citizens of V.F.D. could burn him at the stake, but they still had not arrived in the nick of time.

There are not very many
people in the world who
enjoy delivering bad news,
but I'm sorry to say that Mrs.
Morrow was one of them. When
she caught sight of the Baudelaire orphans gathered around
Jacques, she rushed across
the courtyard to tell them
the details.

"Wait until *The Daily
Punctilio* hears about this!"
she said enthusiastically,

and pointed at Jacques with a sleeve of her pink robe. "Before he could be burned at the stake, Count Omar was murdered mysteriously in his jail cell."

"Count *Olaf*," corrected Violet automatically.

"So you're finally admitting that you know who he is!" she cried triumphantly.

"We don't know who he is!" Klaus insisted, picking up his baby sister, who was quietly beginning to cry. "We only know that he is an innocent man!"

Officer Luciana clunked forward, and the crowd of townspeople and Elders parted to let her walk right up to the children. "I don't think this is a matter for children to discuss," she said, and raised her white-gloved hands in the air to get the crowd's attention.

"Citizens of V.F.D.," she said grandly, "I locked Count Olaf in the uptown jail last night, and when I arrived here in the morning he had been killed. I have the only key to the jail, so his death is quite a mystery."

"A mystery!" Mrs. Morrow said excitedly, as the townspeople murmured behind her. "What a thrill, to be hearing about a mystery!"

"Shoart!" Sunny said tearfully. She meant something like "A dead man is not a thrill!" but only her siblings were listening to her.

"You will all be happy to know that the famous Detective Dupin has agreed to investigate this murder," Officer Luciana continued. "He is inside the uptown jail right now, examining the scene of the crime."

"The famous Detective Dupin!" Mr. Lesko said. "Just imagine!"

"I've never heard of him," said a nearby Elder.

"Me neither," Mr. Lesko admitted, "but I'm sure he's very famous."

"What happened?" Violet asked, trying not to look at the white sheet on the ground. "How was Jacques killed? Why wasn't anybody guarding him? How could someone have gotten into his cell if you locked it?"

Luciana turned around and faced Violet, who could see her own astonished reflection in the policewoman's shiny helmet. "As I said before," Luciana said again, "I don't think this is a matter for children to discuss. Perhaps that man in overalls should take you children to a playground instead of a murder scene."

"Or downtown, to do the morning chores," another Elder said, his crow hat nodding. "Hector, take the orphans away."

"Not so fast," called a voice from the doorway of the uptown jail. It was a voice, I'm sorry to say, that the Baudelaire orphans recognized in an instant. The voice was wheezy, and scratchy, and it had a sinister smile to it, as if the person talking were telling a joke. But it was not a voice that made the children want to laugh at a punch line. It was a voice the children recognized from all of the places they had traveled since their parents had died, and a voice the children knew from all their most displeasing nightmares. It was the voice of Count Olaf.

The children's hearts sank, and they turned to see Olaf standing in the doorway of the jail, wearing another one of his absurd disguises. He was wearing a turquoise blazer that was so brightly colored that it made Baudelaires squint, and a pair of silver pants decorated with tiny mirrors that glinted in the morning sun. A pair of enormous sunglasses covered the entire upper half of his face, hiding his one eyebrow and his shiny, shiny eyes. On his feet were a pair of bright green plastic shoes with yellow plastic lightning bolts sticking out of them, covering his ankle and hiding his tattoo. But most unpleasant of all was the fact that Olaf was wearing no shirt, only a thick gold chain with a detective's badge in the center of it. The Baudelaires could see his pale and hairy chest peeking out at them, and it added an extra layer of unpleasantness to their fear.

"It's just not cool," Count Olaf said, snapping his fingers to emphasize the word "cool," "to dismiss suspects from the scene of the crime until Detective Dupin gives the O.K."

"But surely the orphans aren't suspects," one of the Elders said. "They're only children, after all."

"It's just not cool," Count Olaf said, snapping his fingers again, "to disagree with Detective Dupin."

"I agree," Officer Luciana said, and gave Olaf a big lipstick smile as he stepped through the doorway. "Now let's get down to business, Dupin. Do you have any important information?"

"*We* have some important information," Klaus said boldly. "This man is not Detective Dupin." There were a few gasps from the crowd. "He's Count Olaf."

"You mean Count Omar," Mrs. Morrow said.

"We mean *Olaf*," Violet said, and then turned so that she was looking Count Olaf right in the sunglasses. "Those sunglasses may be hiding your eyebrow, and those shoes may be hiding your tattoo, but you can't hide your identity. You're Count Olaf, and you've kidnapped the Quagmire triplets and murdered Jacques."

"Who in the world is Jacques?" asked an Elder. "I'm confused."

"It's not cool," Olaf said with a snap, "to be confused, so let me see if I can help you." He pointed at himself with a flourish. "I am the famous Detective Dupin. I am wearing these plastic shoes and sunglasses because they're cool. Count Olaf is the name of the man who was murdered last night, and these three children . . ."—here Olaf paused to make sure everyone was listening—"are responsible for the crime."

"Don't be ridiculous, Olaf," Klaus said disgustedly.

Olaf smiled nastily at all three Baudelaires. "You are making a mistake when you call me Count Olaf," he said, "and if you continue to call me that, you will see exactly how big a mistake you are making." Detective Dupin turned and looked up to address the crowd. "Of course, the biggest mistake these children have made is thinking they can get away with murder."

There was a murmur of agreement from the crowd. "I never trusted those kids," Mrs. Morrow said. "They didn't do a very good job when they trimmed my hedges."

"Show them the evidence," Officer Luciana said, and Detective Dupin snapped his fingers.

"It's not cool," he said, "to accuse people of murder without any evidence, but luckily I found some." He reached into the pocket of his blazer and brought out a long pink ribbon decorated with plastic daisies. "I found this right outside Count Olaf's jail cell," he said. "It's a ribbon—the exact kind of ribbon that Violet Baudelaire uses to tie up her hair."

The townspeople gasped, and Violet turned to see that the citizens of V.F.D. were looking at her with suspicion and fear, which are not pleasant ways to be looked at. "That's not my ribbon!" Violet cried, taking her own hair ribbon out of her pocket. "My hair ribbon is right here!"

"How can we tell?" an Elder asked with a frown. "All hair ribbons look alike."

"They don't look alike!" Klaus said. "The one found at the murder scene is fancy and pink. My sister prefers plain ribbons, and she hates the color pink!"

"And inside the cell," Detective Dupin continued, as if Klaus had not spoken, "I found this." He held up a small circle made of glass. "This is one of the lenses in Klaus's glasses."

"But my glasses aren't missing any lenses!" Klaus cried, as everyone turned to look at *him* in suspicion and fear. He took his glasses off and showed them to the crowd. "You can see for yourself."

"Just because you have replaced your ribbon and your lenses," Officer Luciana said, "doesn't mean you're not murderers."

"Actually, they're not murderers," Detective Dupin said. "They're accomplices." He leaned forward so he was right in the Baudelaires' faces, and the children could smell his sour breath as he continued talking. "You orphans are not smart enough to know what the word 'accomplice' means, but it means 'helper of murderers.'"

"We know what the word 'accomplice' means," Klaus said. "What are you talking about?"

"I'm talking about the four toothmarks on Count Olaf's body," Detective Dupin said, with a snap of his fingers. "There's only one person uncool enough to bite people to death, and that's Sunny Baudelaire."

"It's true that her teeth are sharp," another member of the Council said. "I noticed that when she served my hot fudge sundae."

"Our sister didn't bite anyone to death," Violet said indignantly, a word which here means "in defense of an innocent baby." "Detective Dupin is lying!"

"It's not cool to accuse me of lying," Dupin

replied. "Instead of accusing other people of things, why don't you three children tell us where you were last night?"

"We were at Hector's house," Klaus said. "He'll tell you himself." The middle Baudelaire stood up on tiptoe and called out over the crowd. "Hector! Tell everyone that we were with you!"

The citizens looked this way and that, the crow hats of the Elders bobbing as they listened for a word from Hector. But no word came. The three children waited for a moment in the tense silence, thinking that surely Hector would overcome his skittishness in order to save them. But the handyman was quiet. The only sounds the children could hear was the splashing of Fowl Fountain and the muttering of the roosting crows.

"Hector sometimes gets skittish in front of crowds," Violet explained, "but it's true. I spent the night working in his studio, and Klaus was reading in the secret library, and—"

"Enough nonsense!" Officer Luciana said. "Do you really expect us to believe that our fine handyman is building mechanical devices and has a secret library? Next I suppose you'll say that he's building things out of feathers!"

"It's bad enough that you killed Count Olaf," an Elder said, "but now you're trying to frame Hector for other crimes! I say that V.F.D. no longer serve as guardian for such terrible orphans!"

"Hear, hear!" cried several voices scattered in the crowd, just as the children had planned to do themselves.

"I will send a message to Mr. Poe right away," the Elder continued, "and the banker will come and remove them in a few days."

"A few days is too long to wait!" Mrs. Morrow said, and several citizens cheered in agreement. "These children need to be taken care of as quickly as possible."

"I say that we burn them at the stake!" cried Mr. Lesko, who stepped forward to wag his finger at the children. "Rule #201 clearly says no murdering!"

"But we didn't murder anyone!" Violet cried. "A ribbon, a lens, and some bite marks aren't enough evidence to accuse someone of murder!"

"It's enough evidence for me!" an Elder cried. "We already have the torches—let's burn them right now!"

"Hold on a moment," another Elder said. "We can't simply burn people at the stake whenever we want!" The Baudelaires looked at one another, relieved that one citizen seemed immune to mob psychology. "I have a very important appointment in ten minutes," the Elder continued. "So it's too late to do it now. How about tonight, after dinner?"

"That's no good," said another member of the Council. "I'm having a dinner party then. How about tomorrow afternoon?"

"Yes," someone said from the crowd. "Right after lunch! That's a perfect time!"

"Hear, hear!" Mr. Lesko cried.

"Hear, hear!" Mrs. Morrow cried.

"Glaji!" Sunny cried.

"Hector, help us!" Violet called. "Please tell these people that we're not murderers!"

"I told you before," Detective Dupin said, smiling beneath his sunglasses. "Only Sunny is a murderer. You two are accomplices, and I will put you all in jail where you belong." Dupin grabbed Violet's and Klaus's wrists with one scraggly hand, and leaned down to scoop up Sunny with the other. "See you tomorrow afternoon for the burning at the stake!" he called out to the rest of the crowd, and dragged the struggling Baudelaires through the door of the uptown jail. The children stumbled into a dim, grim hallway, listening to the faint sounds of the mob cheering as the door slammed behind them.

"I'm putting you in the Deluxe Cell,"

Dupin said. "It's the dirtiest one." He marched them down a dark hallway with many twists and turns, and the Baudelaires could see rows and rows of cells with their heavy doors hanging open. The only light in the jail came from tiny barred windows placed in each cell, but the children saw that every cell was empty and each one looked dirtier than the rest.

"You'll be the one in jail before long, Olaf," Klaus said, hoping he sounded much more certain than he felt. "You'll never get away with this."

"My name is Detective Dupin," said Detective Dupin, "and my only concern is bringing you three criminals to justice."

"But if you burn us at the stake," Violet said quickly, "you'll never get your hands on the Baudelaire fortune."

Dupin rounded the last corner of the hallway, and pushed the Baudelaires into a small damp cell with only a small wooden bench as furniture. By the light of the barred window, the siblings could see that the cell was quite filthy, as Dupin had promised. The detective reached out to pull the door closed, but with his sunglasses on it was too dark to see the door handle, so he had to throw off all pretense—a phrase which here means "take off part of his disguise for a moment"—and remove his sunglasses. As much as the children hated Dupin's ridiculous disguise, it was worse to see their enemy's one eyebrow, and the shiny, shiny eyes that had been haunting them for so long.

"Don't worry," he said in his wheezy voice. "You won't be burned at the stake—not all of you, at least. Tomorrow afternoon, one of you will make a miraculous escape—if you consider being smuggled out of V.F.D. by one of my assistants to be an escape. The other two will burn at the stake as planned. You bratty orphans are too stupid to realize it, but a genius like me knows that it may take a village to raise a child, but it only takes one child to inherit a fortune." The villain laughed a loud and rude laugh, and began to shut the door of the cell. "But I don't want to be cruel," he said, smiling to indicate that he really wanted to be as cruel as possible. "I'll let you three decide who gets the honor of spending the rest of their puny life with me, and who gets to burn at the stake. I'll be back at lunchtime for your decision."

The Baudelaire orphans listened to the wheezy giggle of their enemy as he slammed the cell door and walked back down the hallway in his plastic shoes, and felt a sinking feeling in their stomachs, where the huevos rancheros Hector had made for them last night were still being digested. When something is being digested, of course, it is getting smaller and smaller as the body uses up all of the nutrients inside the food, but it didn't feel that way to the three children. The youngsters did not feel as if the small potatoes they had eaten for dinner were getting smaller. The Baudelaire orphans huddled together in the dim light and listened to the laughter echo against the walls of the uptown jail, and wondered just how large the potatoes of their lives would grow.

Entertaining a notion, like entertaining a baby cousin or entertaining a pack of hyenas, is a dangerous thing to refuse to do. If you refuse to entertain a baby cousin, the baby cousin may get bored and entertain itself by wandering off and falling down a well. If you refuse to entertain a pack of hyenas, they may become restless and entertain themselves by devouring you. But if you refuse to entertain a notion—which is just a fancy way of saying that you refuse to think about a certain idea—you have to be much braver than someone who is merely facing some bloodthirsty animals, or some parents who are

upset to find their little darling at the bottom of
a well, because nobody knows what an idea will
do when it goes off to entertain itself, particularly if the idea comes from a sinister villain.

"I don't care what that horrible man says,"
Violet said to her siblings as Detective Dupin's
plastic footsteps faded away. "We're not going
to choose which one of us will escape and who
will be left to burn at the stake. I absolutely
refuse to entertain the notion."

"But what are we going to do?" Klaus asked.
"Try to contact Mr. Poe?"

"Mr. Poe won't help us," Violet replied.
"He'll think we're ruining the reputation of his
bank. We're going to escape."

"Frulk!" Sunny said.

"I know it's a jail cell," Violet said, "but
there must be some way to get out." She pulled
her ribbon out of her pocket and tied up her
hair, her fingers shaking as she did so. The
eldest Baudelaire had spoken confidently, but

she did not feel as confident as she sounded. A cell is built for the specific purpose of keeping people inside, and she was not sure she could make an invention that could get the Baudelaires out of the uptown jail. But once her hair was out of her eyes, her inventing brain began to work at full force, and Violet took a good look around the cell for ideas. First she looked at the door of the cell, examining every inch of it.

"Do you think you could make another lockpick?" Klaus asked hopefully. "You made an excellent one when we lived with Uncle Monty."

"Not this time," Violet replied. "The door locks from the outside, so a lockpick would be of no use." She closed her eyes for a moment in thought, and then looked up at the tiny barred window. Her siblings followed her gaze, a phrase which here means "also looked at the window and tried to think of something helpful."

"Boiklio?" Sunny asked, which meant "Do you think you could make some more welding torches, to melt the bars? You made some excellent ones when we lived with the Squalors."

"Not this time," Violet said. "If I stood on the bench and Klaus stood on my shoulders and you stood on Klaus's shoulders, we could probably reach the window, but even if we melted the bars, the window isn't big enough to crawl through, even for Sunny."

"Sunny could call out the window," Klaus said, "and try to attract the attention of someone to come and save us."

"Thanks to mob psychology, every citizen of V.F.D. thinks that we're criminals," Violet pointed out. "No one is going to come rescue an accused murderer and her accomplices." She closed her eyes and thought again, and then knelt down to get a closer look at the wooden bench.

"Rats," she said.

Klaus jumped slightly. "Where?" he said.

"I don't mean there are rats in the cell," she said, hoping that she was speaking the truth. "I just mean 'Rats!' I was hoping that the bench would be made of wooden boards held together with screws or nails. Screws and nails are always handy for inventions. But it's just a solid, carved piece of wood, which isn't handy at all." Violet sat down on the solid, carved piece of wood and sighed. "I don't know what I can do," she admitted.

Klaus and Sunny looked at one another nervously. "I'm sure you'll think of something," Klaus said.

"Maybe *you'll* think of something," Violet replied, looking at her brother. "There must be something you've read that could help us."

It was Klaus's turn to close his eyes in thought. "If you tilted the bench," he said, after a pause, "it would become a ramp. The ancient Egyptians used ramps to build the pyramids."

"But we're not trying to build a pyramid!" Violet cried in exasperation. "We're trying to escape from jail!"

"I'm just trying to be helpful!" Klaus cried.

"If it weren't for you and your silly hair ribbons, we wouldn't have been arrested in the first place!"

"And if it weren't for your ridiculous glasses," Violet snapped in reply, "we wouldn't be here in this jail!"

"Stop!" Sunny shrieked.

Violet and Klaus glared angrily at one another for a moment, and then sighed. Violet moved over on the bench to make room for her siblings.

"Come and sit down," she said gloomily. "I'm sorry I yelled at you, Klaus. Of course it's not your fault that we're here."

"It's not yours, either," Klaus said. "I'm just frustrated. Only a few hours ago we thought we'd be able to find the Quagmires and save Jacques."

"But we were too late to save Jacques," Violet said, shuddering. "I don't know who he was, or how he got his tattoo, but I know he wasn't Count Olaf."

"Maybe he used to work with Count Olaf," Klaus said. "He said the tattoo was from his job. Do you think Jacques was in Olaf's theater troupe?"

"I don't think so," Violet said. "None of Olaf's associates have that same tattoo. If only Jacques were alive, he could solve the mystery."

"Pereg," Sunny said, which meant "And if only the Quagmires were here, they could solve the other mystery—the meaning of the real V.F.D."

"What we need," Klaus said, "is deus ex machina."

"Who's that?" Violet said.

"It's not a who," Klaus said, "it's a what. 'Deus ex machina' is a Latin term that means 'the god from the machine.' It means the arrival of something helpful when you least expect it. We need to rescue two triplets from the clutches of a villain, and solve the sinister mystery surrounding us, but we're trapped in the filthiest cell of the uptown jail, and tomorrow afternoon we're supposed to be burned at the stake. It would be a wonderful time for something helpful to arrive unexpectedly."

At that moment there was a knock on the door, and the sound of the lock unlatching. The heavy door of the Deluxe Cell creaked open, and there stood Officer Luciana, scowling at them from beneath the visor of her helmet and holding a loaf of bread in one hand and a pitcher of water in the other. "If it were up to me, I wouldn't be doing this," she said, "but Rule #141 clearly states that all prisoners receive bread and water, so here you go." The Chief of Police thrust the loaf and the pitcher into Violet's hands and slammed the door shut, locking it behind her. Violet stared at the loaf of bread, which looked spongy and unappetizing, and at the water pitcher, which was decorated with a painting of seven crows flying in a circle. "Well, at least we have some nourishment," she said. "Our brains need food and water to work properly."

She handed the pitcher to Sunny and the loaf to Klaus, who looked at the bread for a long, long time. Then, he turned to his sisters, who could see that his eyes were filling up with tears.

"I just remembered," he said, in a quiet, sad voice. "It's my birthday. I'm thirteen today."

Violet put her hand on her brother's shoulder. "Oh, Klaus," she said. "It *is* your birthday. We forgot all about it."

"I forgot all about it myself, until this very moment," Klaus said, looking back at the loaf of bread. "Something about this bread made me remember my twelfth birthday, when our parents made that bread pudding."

Violet put the pitcher of water down on the floor, and sat beside Klaus. "I remember," she said, smiling. "That was the worst dessert we ever tasted."

"Vom," Sunny agreed.

"It was a new recipe that they were trying out," Klaus said. "They wanted it to be special for my birthday, but it was burned and sour and soggy. And they promised that the next year, for my thirteenth birthday, I'd have the best birthday meal in the world." He looked at his siblings, and had to take his glasses off to wipe away his tears. "I don't mean to sound spoiled," he said, "but I was hoping for a better birthday meal than bread and water in the Deluxe Cell of the uptown jail in the Village of Fowl Devotees."

"Chift," Sunny said, biting Klaus's hand gently.

Violet hugged him, and felt her own eyes fill up with tears as well. "Sunny's right, Klaus. You don't sound spoiled."

The Baudelaires sat together for a moment and cried quietly, entertaining the notion of how dreadful their lives had become in such a short time. Klaus's twelfth birthday did not seem like such a long time ago, and yet their memories of the lousy bread pudding seemed as faint and blurry as their first sight of V.F.D. on the horizon. It was a curious feeling, that something could be so close and so distant at the same time, and the children wept for their mother and their father and all of the happy things in their life that had been taken away from them since that terrible day at the beach.

Finally, the children cried themselves out, and Violet wiped her eyes and struggled to give her brother a smile. "Klaus," she said, "Sunny and I are prepared to offer you the birthday gift of your choice. Anything at all that you want in the Deluxe Cell, you can have."

"Thanks a lot," Klaus said, smiling as he looked around the filthy room. "What I'd really like is deus ex machina."

"Me, too," Violet agreed, and took the pitcher of water from her sister to drink from it. Before she even took a sip, however, she looked up, and stared at the far end of the cell. Putting down the pitcher, she quickly walked to the wall and rubbed some dirt away to see what the wall was made of. Then looked at her siblings and began to smile. "Happy birthday, Klaus," she said. "Officer Luciana brought us deus ex machina."

"She didn't bring us a god in a machine," Klaus said. "She brought water in a pitcher."

"Brioche!" Sunny said, which meant "And bread!"

"They're the closest thing to a god in a machine that we're going to get," Violet said. "Now get up, both of you. We need the bench—it'll be handy after all. It's going to work as a ramp, just as Klaus said."

Violet placed the loaf of bread up against the wall, directly under the barred window, and then tilted the bench toward the same spot. "We're going to pour the pitcher of water so it runs down the bench, and hits the wall," she said. "Then it'll run down the wall to the bread, which will act like a sponge and soak up the water. Then we'll squeeze the bread so the water goes into the pitcher, and start over."

"But what will that do?" Klaus asked.

"The walls of this cell are made of bricks," Violet said, "with mortar between the bricks to keep them together. Mortar is a type of clay that hardens like glue, so a mortar-dissolver would loosen the bricks and allow us to escape. I think we can dissolve the mortar by pouring water on it."

"But how?" Klaus asked. "The walls are so solid, and water is so gentle."

"Water is one of the most powerful forces on earth," Violet replied. "Ocean waves can wear away at cliffs made of stone."

"Donax!" Sunny said, which meant something like, "But that takes years and years, and if we don't escape, we'll be burned at the stake tomorrow afternoon."

"Then we'd better stop entertaining the notion, and start pouring the water," Violet said. "We'll have to keep it up all night if we want to dissolve the mortar. I'll stand at this end, propping up the bench. Klaus, you stand next to me and pour the water. Sunny, you stand near the bread, and bring it back to me when it's soaked up all the water. Ready?"

Klaus took the pitcher in his hands and held it up to the end of the bench. Sunny crawled over to the loaf of bread, which was only a little bit shorter than she was. "Ready!" the two younger Baudelaires said in unison, and together the three children began to operate Violet's mortar-dissolver. The water ran down the bench and hit the wall, and then ran down the wall and was soaked up in the spongy bread. Sunny quickly brought the bread to Klaus, who squeezed it into the pitcher, and the entire process began again. At first, it seemed as if the Baudelaires were barking up the wrong tree, because the water seemed to have no more effect against the wall of the Deluxe Cell than a silk scarf would have against a charging rhinoceros, but it soon became clear that water—unlike a silk scarf—is indeed one of the most powerful forces on earth. By the time the Baudelaires heard the flapping of the V.F.D. crows as they flew in a circle before heading downtown for their afternoon roost, the mortar between the bricks was slightly mushy to the touch, and by the time the last few rays of the sun were shining through the tiny barred window, quite a bit of the mortar had actually begun to wear away.

"Grespo," Sunny said, which meant something like, "Quite a bit of the mortar has actually begun to wear away."

"That's good news," Klaus said. "If your invention saves our lives, Violet, it will be the best birthday present you've ever given me, including that book of Finnish poetry you bought me when I turned eight."

Violet yawned. "Speaking of poetry, why don't we talk about Isadora Quagmire's couplets? We still haven't figured out where the triplets are hidden, and besides, if we keep talking it'll be easier to stay awake."

"Good idea," Klaus said, and recited the poems from memory:

> *"For sapphires we are held in here.*
> *Only you can end our fear.*
>
> *Until dawn comes we cannot speak.*
> *No words can come from this sad beak.*
>
> *The first thing you read contains the clue:*
> *An initial way to speak to you."*

The Baudelaires listened to the poems and began to entertain every notion they could think of that might help them figure out what the couplets meant. Violet held the bench in place, but her mind was on why the first poem began "For sapphires we are held in here," when the Baudelaires already knew about the Quagmire fortune. Klaus poured the water out of the pitcher and let it run down to the wall, but his mind was on the part of the poem that said "The first thing you read contains the clue," and what exactly Isadora meant by "the clue." Sunny monitored the loaf of bread as it soaked up the water again and again, but her mind was on the last line of the last poem they had received, and what "An initial way to speak to you" could mean. The three Baudelaires operated Violet's invention until morning, discussing Isadora's couplets the entire time, and although the children made quite a lot of progress dissolving the mortar in the cell wall, they made no progress figuring out Isadora's poems.

"Water might be one of the most powerful forces on earth," Violet said, as the children heard the first sounds of the V.F.D. crows arriving for their uptown roost, "but poetry might be the most confusing. We've talked and talked, and we still don't know where the Quagmires are hiding."

"We need another dose of deus ex machina," Klaus said. "If something helpful doesn't arrive soon, we won't be able to rescue our friends, even if we do escape from this cell."

"Psst!" came an unexpected voice from the window, startling the children so much that they almost dropped everything and wrecked the mortar-dissolver. The Baudelaires looked up and saw the faint shape of somebody's face behind the bars of the window. "Psst! Baudelaires!" the voice whispered.

"Who is it?" Violet whispered back. "We can't see you."

"It's Hector," Hector whispered. "I'm supposed to be downtown doing the morning chores, but I sneaked over here instead."

"Can you get us out of here?" Klaus whispered.

For a few seconds, the children heard nothing but the sounds of the V.F.D. crows muttering and splashing in Fowl Fountain. Then Hector sighed. "No," he admitted. "Officer Luciana has the only key, and this jail is made of solid brick. I don't think there's a way I can get you out."

"Dala?" Sunny asked.

"My sister means, did you tell the Council of Elders that we were with you the night Jacques was murdered, so we couldn't have committed the crime?"

There was another pause. "No," Hector said. "You know that the Council makes me too skittish to talk. I wanted to speak up for you when Detective Dupin was accusing you, but one look at those crow hats and I couldn't open my mouth. But I thought of one thing I can do to help."

Klaus put down the pitcher of water and felt the mortar on the far wall. Violet's invention seemed to be working quite well, but there was still no guarantee that it would get them out of there before the mob of citizens arrived in the afternoon. "What's that?" he asked Hector.

"I'm going to get the self-sustaining hot air

mobile home ready to go," he said. "I'll wait at the barn all afternoon, and if you somehow manage to escape, you can float away with me."

"O.K.," Violet said, although she had been hoping for something a little more helpful from a fully grown adult. "We're trying to break out of this cell right now, so maybe we'll make it."

"Well, if you're breaking out now, I'd better go," Hector said. "I don't want to get in trouble. I just want to say that if you don't make it and you are burned at the stake, it was very nice making your acquaintance. Oh—I almost forgot."

Hector's fingers reached through the bars and dropped a rolled scrap of paper down to the waiting Baudelaires. "It's another couplet," he said. "It doesn't make sense to me, but maybe you'll find it helpful. Good-bye, children. I do hope I see you later."

"Good-bye, Hector," Violet said glumly. "I hope so too."

"'Bye," Sunny muttered.

Hector waited for a second, expecting Klaus to say good-bye, but then walked off without another word, his footsteps fading into the sounds of the muttering, splashing crows. Violet and Sunny turned to look at their brother, surprised that he had not said good-bye, although Hector's visit had been such a disappointment that they could understand if Klaus was too annoyed to be polite. But when they looked at the middle Baudelaire, he did not look annoyed. Klaus was looking at the latest couplet from Isadora, and in the growing light of the Deluxe Cell his sisters could see a wide grin on his face. Grinning is something you do when you are entertained in some way, such as reading a good book or watching someone you don't care for spill orange soda all over himself. But there weren't any books in the uptown jail, and the Baudelaires had been careful not to spill a drop of the water as they operated the mortar-dissolver, so the Baudelaire sisters knew that their brother was grinning for another reason.

He was grinning because he was entertaining a notion, and as Klaus showed them the poem he was holding, Violet and Sunny had a very good idea of what notion it was.

CHAPTER Eleven

*Inside these letters, the eye will see
Nearby are your friends, and V.F.D.*

"*Isn't* it marvelous?" Klaus said with a grin, as his sisters read the fourth couplet. "Isn't it absolutely superlative?"

"Wibeon," Sunny said, which meant "It's more confusing than superlative—we still don't know where the Quagmires are."

"Yes we do," Klaus said, taking the other couplets out of his pocket.

"Think about all four poems in order, and you'll see what I mean."

> *For sapphires we are held in here.*
> *Only you can end our fear.*
>
> *Until dawn comes we cannot speak.*
> *No words can come from this sad beak.*
>
> *The first thing you read contains the clue:*
> *An initial way to speak to you.*
>
> *Inside these letters the eye will see*
> *Nearby are your friends, and V.F.D.*

"I think you're much better at analyzing poetry than I am," Violet said, and Sunny nodded in agreement. "This poem doesn't make it any clearer."

"But you're the one who first suggested the solution," Klaus said. "When we received the third poem, you thought that 'initial' meant 'initials,' like V.F.D."

"But you said that it probably meant 'first,'" Violet said. "The poems are the first way the Quagmires can speak to us from where they are hidden."

"I was wrong," Klaus admitted. "I've never been so happy to be wrong in my life. Isadora meant 'initials' all along. I didn't realize it until I read the part that said 'Inside these letters the eye will see.' She's hiding the location inside the poem, like Aunt Josephine hid her location inside her note, remember?"

"Of course I remember," Violet said, "but I still don't understand."

"'The first thing you read contains the clue,'" Klaus recited. "We thought that Isadora meant the first poem. But she meant the first *letter*. She couldn't tell us directly where she and her brother were hidden, in case someone else got the poems from the crows before we did, so she had to use a sort of code. If we look at the first letter of each line, and we can see the triplets' location."

"'For sapphires we are held in here.' That's F," Violet said. "'Only you can end our fear.' That's O."

"'Until dawn comes we cannot speak,'" Klaus said. "That's U. 'No words can come from this sad beak.' That's N."

"'The first thing you read contains the clue'—T," Violet said excitedly. "'An initial way to speak to you'—A."

"I! N!" Sunny cried triumphantly, and the three Baudelaires cried out the solution together: "FOUNTAIN!"

"Fowl Fountain!" Klaus said. "The Quagmires are right outside that window."

"But how can they be in the fountain?" Violet asked. "And how could Isadora give her poems to the V.F.D. crows?"

"We'll answer those questions," Klaus

replied, "as soon as we get out of jail. We'd better get back to the mortar-dissolver before Detective Dupin comes back."

"Along with a whole town of people who want to burn us at the stake, thanks to mob psychology," Violet said with a shudder.

Sunny crawled over to the loaf of bread and placed her tiny hand against the wall. "Mush!" she cried, which meant something like, "The mortar is almost dissolved—just a little bit longer!"

Violet took the ribbon out of her hair and then retied it, which was something she did when she needed to rethink, a word which here means "Think even harder about the Baudelaire orphans' terrible situation." "I'm not sure we have even a little bit longer," she said, looking up at the window. "Look at how bright the sunlight is. The morning must be almost over."

"Then we should hurry," Klaus said.

"No," Violet corrected. "We should rethink.

And I've been rethinking this bench. We can use it in another way, besides as a ramp. We can use it as a battering ram."

"Honz?" Sunny asked.

"A battering ram is a large piece of wood or metal used to break down doors or walls," Violet explained. "Military inventors used it in medieval times to break into walled cities, and we're going to use it now, to break out of jail." Violet picked up the bench so it was resting on her shoulder. "The bench should be pointing as evenly as possible," she said. "Sunny, get on Klaus's shoulders. If the two of you hold the other end together, I think this battering ram will work."

Klaus and Sunny scrambled into the position Violet had suggested, and in a moment the siblings were ready to operate Violet's latest invention. The two Baudelaire sisters had a firm hold on the wood, and Klaus had a firm hold on Sunny so she wouldn't fall to the floor of the Deluxe Cell as they battered.

"Now," Violet said, "let's step back as far as we can, and at the count of three, run quickly toward the wall. Aim the battering ram for the spot where the mortar-dissolver was working. Ready? One, two, *three!*"

Thunk! The Baudelaires ran forward and smacked the bench against the wall as hard as they could. The battering ram made a noise so loud that it felt as if the entire jail would collapse, but they left only a small dent in a few of the bricks, as if the wall had been bruised slightly. "Again!" Violet commanded. "One, two, *three!*"

Thunk! Outside the children could hear a few crows flutter wildly, frightened by the noise. A few more bricks were bruised, and one had a long crack down the middle. "It's working!" Klaus cried. "The battering ram is working!"

"One, two, *minga!*" Sunny shrieked, and the children smacked the battering ram against the wall again.

"Ow!" Klaus cried, and stumbled a little bit,

almost dropping his baby sister. "A brick fell on my toe!"

"Hooray!" Violet cried. "I mean, sorry about your toe, Klaus, but if bricks are falling it means the wall is definitely weakening. Let's put down the battering ram and get a better look."

"We don't need a better look," Klaus said. "We'll know it's working when we see Fowl Fountain. One, two, *three!*"

Thunk! The Baudelaires heard the sound of more pieces of brick hitting the filthy floor of the Deluxe Cell. But they also heard another sound—a familiar one. It began with a faint rustling, and then grew and grew until it sounded like a million pages were being flipped. It was the sound of the V.F.D. crows, flying in circles before departing for their afternoon roost, and it meant that the children were running out of time.

"Hurol!" Sunny cried desperately, and then, as loudly as she could, "One! Two! *Minga!*"

At the count of "Minga!" which of course

meant something along the lines of "Three!" the children raced toward the wall of the Deluxe Cell and smacked their battering ram against the bricks with the mightiest *Thunk!* yet, a noise that was accompanied by an enormous cracking sound as the invention snapped in two. Violet staggered in one direction, and Klaus and Sunny staggered in another, as each separate half made them lose their balance, and a huge cloud of dust sprang from the point where the battering ram had hit the wall.

A huge cloud of dust is not a beautiful thing to look at. Very few painters have done portraits of huge clouds of dust or included them in their landscapes or still lifes. Film directors rarely choose huge clouds of dust to play the lead roles in romantic comedies, and as far as my research has shown, a huge cloud of dust has never placed higher than twenty-fifth in a beauty pageant. Nevertheless, as the Baudelaire orphans stumbled around the cell, dropping each half of the battering ram and listening to the sound of the crows flying in circles outside, they stared at the huge cloud of dust as if it were a thing of great beauty, because this particular huge dust cloud was made of pieces of brick and mortar and other building materials that are needed to build a wall, and the Baudelaires knew that they were seeing it because Violet's invention had worked. As the huge cloud of dust settled on the cell floor, making it even dirtier, the children gazed around them with big dusty grins on their faces, because they saw an additional beautiful sight—a big, gaping hole in the wall of the Deluxe Cell, perfect for a speedy escape.

"We did it!" Violet said, and stepped through the hole in the cell into the courtyard. She looked up at the sky just in time to see the last few crows departing for the downtown district. "We escaped!"

Klaus, still holding Sunny on his shoulders, paused to wipe the dust off his glasses before stepping out of the cell and walking past Violet to Fowl Fountain. "We're not out of the woods yet," he said, using a phrase which here means "There's still plenty of trouble on the horizon." He looked up at the sky and pointed to the distant blur of the departing crows. "The crows are heading downtown for their afternoon roost. The townspeople should arrive any minute now."

"But how can we get the Quagmires out any minute now?" Violet asked.

"Wock!" Sunny cried from Klaus's shoulders. She meant something like, "The fountain looks as solid as can be," and her siblings nodded in disappointed agreement. Fowl Fountain looked as impenetrable—a word which here means "impossible to break into and rescue kidnapped triplets"—as it did ugly. The metal crow sat and spat water all over itself as if the idea of the Baudelaires rescuing the Quagmires made it sick to its stomach.

"Duncan and Isadora must be trapped inside

the fountain," Klaus said. "Perhaps there's a mechanism someplace that opens up a secret entrance."

"But we cleaned every inch of this fountain for our afternoon chores," Violet said. "We would have noticed a secret mechanism while we were scrubbing all those carved feathers."

"Jidu!" Sunny said, which meant something like, "Surely Isadora has given us a hint about how to rescue her!"

Klaus put down his baby sister, and took the four scraps of paper out of his pocket. "It's time to rethink again," he said, spreading out the couplets on the ground. "We need to examine these poems as closely as we can. There must be another clue about getting into the fountain."

> *For sapphires we are held in here.*
> *Only you can end our fear.*
>
> *Until dawn comes we cannot speak.*
> *No words can come from this sad beak.*

The first thing you read contains the clue:
An initial way to speak to you.

Inside these letters the eye will see
Nearby are your friends, and V.F.D.

"'*This sad beak*'!" Violet exclaimed. "We jumped to the conclusion that she meant the V.F.D. crows, but maybe she means Fowl Fountain. The water comes out of the crow's beak, so there must be a hole there."

"We'd better climb up and see," Klaus said. "Here, Sunny, get on my shoulders again, and then I'll get on Violet's shoulders. We're going to have to be very tall to reach all the way up there."

Violet nodded, and knelt at the base of the fountain. Klaus put Sunny back on his shoulders, and then got on the shoulders of his older sister, and then carefully, carefully, Violet stood up, so all three Baudelaires were balancing on top of one another like a troupe of acrobats the children had seen once when their parents had taken them to the circus. The key difference, however, is that acrobats rehearse their routines over and over, in rooms with safety nets and plenty of cushions so that when they make a mistake they will not injure themselves, but the Baudelaire orphans had no time to rehearse, or to find cushions to lay out on V.F.D.'s streets. As a result, the Baudelaire balancing act was a wobbly one. Violet wobbled from holding up both her siblings, and Klaus wobbled from standing on his wobbling sister, and poor Sunny was wobbling so much that she was just barely able to sit up on Klaus's shoulder and peer into the beak of the gargling metal crow. Violet looked down the street, to watch for any arriving townspeople, and Klaus gazed down at the ground, where Isadora's poems were still spread out.

"What do you see, Sunny?" asked Violet, who had spotted a few very distant figures walking quickly toward the fountain.

"Shize!" Sunny called down.

"Klaus, the beak isn't big enough to get inside the fountain," Violet said desperately. The streets of the town appeared to be shaking up and down as she wobbled more and more. "What can we do?"

"'Inside these letters the eye will see,'" Klaus muttered to himself, as he often did when he was thinking hard about something he was reading. It took all of his concentration to read the couplets Isadora had sent them while he was teetering back and forth. "That's a strange way to put it. Why didn't she write 'Inside these letters I hope you'll see,' or 'Inside these letters you just might see'?"

"Sabisho!" Sunny cried. From the top of her two wobbling siblings, Sunny was waving back and forth like a flower in the breeze. She tried to hang on to Fowl Fountain, but the water rushing out of the crow's beak made the metal too slippery.

Violet tried as hard as she could to steady herself, but the sight of two figures wearing crow-shaped hats coming around a nearby corner did not help her find her balance. "Klaus," she said, "I don't mean to rush you, but please rethink as quickly as you can. The citizens are approaching, and I'm not sure how much longer I can hang on."

"'Inside these letters the eye will see,'" Klaus muttered again, closing his eyes so he wouldn't have to see the world wobbling around him.

"Took!" Sunny shrieked, but no one heard her over Violet's scream as her legs gave out, a phrase which here means that she toppled to the ground, skinning her knee and dropping Klaus in the process. Klaus's glasses dropped off, and he fell to the ground of the courtyard elbows first, which is a painful way to fall, and as he rolled on the ground both of his elbows received nasty scrapes. But Klaus was far more concerned about his hands, which were no longer clasping the feet of his baby sister. "Sunny!" he called, squinting without his glasses. "Sunny, where are you?"

"Heni!" Sunny screamed, but it was even more difficult than usual to understand what she meant. The youngest Baudelaire had managed to cling to the beak of the crow with her teeth, but as the fountain kept spitting out water, her mouth began to slip off the slick metal surface. "Heni!" she screamed again, as one of her upper teeth started to slip. Sunny began to slide down, down, scrambling desperately to find something to hang on to, but the only other feature carved into the head was the staring eye of the crow, which was flat and provided no sort of toothhold. She slipped down farther, farther, and Sunny closed her eyes rather than watch herself fall.

"Heni!" she screamed one last time, gnashing her teeth against the eye in frustration, and as she bit the eye, it depressed. "Depressed" is a word that often describes someone who is feeling sad and gloomy, but in this case it describes a secret button, hidden in a crow statue, that is feeling just fine, thank you. With a great creaking noise, the button depressed and the beak of Fowl Fountain opened as wide as it could, each part of the beak flipping slowly down and bringing Sunny down with it. Klaus found his glasses and put them on just in time to see his little sister drop safely into Violet's outstretched arms. The three Baudelaires looked at one another with relief, and then looked at the widening beak of the crow. Through the rushing water, the three siblings could see two pairs of hands appear on the beak as two people climbed out of Fowl Fountain. Each person was wearing a thick wool sweater, so dark and heavy with water that they both looked like huge, mis-shapen monsters. The two dripping figures climbed carefully out of the crow and lowered themselves to the ground, and the Baudelaires ran to clasp them in their arms.

I do not have to tell you how overjoyed the children were to see Duncan and Isadora Quagmire shivering in the courtyard, and I do not have to tell you how grateful the Quagmires were to be out of the confines of Fowl Fountain. I do not have to tell you how happy and relieved the five youngsters were to be reunited after all this time, and I do not have to tell you all the joyous things the triplets said as they struggled to take off their heavy sweaters and wring them out. But there are things I do have to tell you, and one of those things is the distant figure of Detective Dupin, holding a torch and heading straight toward the Baudelaire orphans.

CHAPTER

Twelve

If you have reached this far in the story, you must stop now. If you take one step back and look at the book you are reading, you can see how little of this miserable story there is to go, but if you could know how much grief and woe are contained in these last few pages, you would take another step back, and then another, and keep stepping back until *The Vile Village* was just as small and distant as the approaching figure of Detective Dupin was as the Baudelaire orphans embraced their friends in relief and joy. The Baudelaire orphans, I'm sorry to say, could not stop now, and there is no way for me to travel backward in time and warn the Baudelaires that the relief and joy they were experiencing at Fowl Fountain were the last bits of relief and joy they would experience for a very long time. But I can warn you. You, unlike the Baudelaire orphans and the Quagmire triplets and me and my dear departed Beatrice, can stop this wretched story at this very moment, and see what happens at the end of *The Littlest Elf* instead.

"We can't stay here," Violet warned. "I don't mean to cut short this reunion, but it's already afternoon, and Detective Dupin is coming down that street."

The five children looked in the direction Violet was pointing, and could see the turquoise speck of Dupin's approaching blazer, and the tiny point of light his flaming torch made as he drew near the courtyard.

"Do you think he sees us?" Klaus asked.

"I don't know," Violet said, "but let's not stick around to find out. The V.F.D. mob will only get worse when they discover we've broken out of jail."

"Detective Dupin is the latest disguise of Count Olaf," Klaus explained to the Quagmires, "and—"

"We know all about Detective Dupin," Duncan said quickly, "and we know what's happened to you."

"We heard everything that happened yesterday, from inside the fountain," Isadora said. "When we heard you cleaning the fountain we tried to make as much noise as we could, but you couldn't hear *us* over the sound of all that water."

Duncan squeezed a whole puddle out of the soaked stitches of his left sweater sleeve. Then he reached under his shirt and brought out a dark green notebook. "We tried to keep our notebooks as dry as possible," he explained. "After all, there's crucial information in here."

"We have all the information about V.F.D.," Isadora said, taking out her notebook, which was pitch black. "The real V.F.D., that is, not the Village of Fowl Devotees."

Duncan opened his notebook and blew on some of the damp pages. "And we know the complete story of poor Jac—"

Duncan was interrupted by a shriek behind him, and the five children turned to see two members of the Council of Elders staring at the hole in the uptown jail. Quickly, the Baudelaires and Quagmires ducked behind Fowl Fountain so they wouldn't be seen.

One of the Elders shrieked again, and removed his crow hat to dab at his brow with a tissue. "They've escaped!" he cried. "Rule #1,742 clearly states that no one is allowed to escape from jail. How dare they disobey this rule!"

"We should have expected this from a murderer and her two accomplices," the other Elder said. "And look—they've damaged Fowl Fountain. The beak is split wide open. Our beautiful fountain is ruined!"

"Those three orphans are the worst criminals in history," the first replied. "Look—there's
Detective Dupin, walking down that street.
Let's go tell him what's happened. Maybe he'll
figure out where they've gone."

"You go tell Dupin," the second Elder said,
"and I'll go call *The Daily Punctilio*. Maybe
they'll put my name in the newspaper."

The two members of the Council hurried off
to spread the news, and the children sighed in
relief. "Cose," Sunny said.

"That was *too* close," Klaus replied. "Soon
this whole district will be full of citizens hunting us down."

"Well, nobody's hunting *us*," Duncan said.
"Isadora and I will walk in front of you, so you
won't be spotted."

"But where can we go?" Isadora asked.
"This vile village is in the middle of nowhere."

"I helped Hector finish his self-sustaining
hot air mobile home," Violet said, "and he
promised to have it waiting for us. All we have

to do is make it to the outskirts of town, and we can escape."

"And live forever up in the air?" Klaus said, frowning.

"Maybe it won't be forever," Violet replied.

"Scylla!" Sunny said, which meant "It's either the self-sustaining hot air mobile home, or being burned at the stake!"

"When you say it like that," Klaus said, "I'm convinced."

Everyone agreed, and Violet looked around the courtyard to see if anyone else had arrived yet. "In a place as flat as this one," she said, "you can see people coming from far away, and we're going to use that to our advantage. We'll walk along any empty street we can find, and if we see anyone coming, we'll turn a corner. We won't be able to get there as the crow flies, but eventually we'll be able to reach Nevermore Tree."

"Speaking of the crows," Klaus said to the two triplets, "how did you manage to deliver those poems by crow? And how did you know that we would receive them?"

"Let's get moving," Isadora replied. "We'll tell you the whole story as we go along."

The five children got moving. With the Quagmire triplets in the lead, the group of youngsters peered down one street after another until they found one without a sign of anyone coming, and hurried out of the courtyard.

"Olaf smuggled us away in that item from the In Auction with the help of Esmé Squalor," Duncan began, referring to the last time the Baudelaires had seen him and his sister. "And he hid us for a while in the tower room of his terrible house."

Violet shuddered. "I haven't thought of that room in quite some time," she said. "It's hard to believe that we used to live with such a vile man."

Klaus pointed to the distant figure who was walking toward them, and the five children turned onto another empty street. "This street doesn't lead to Hector's house," he said, "but we'll try to double back. Go on, Duncan."

"Olaf learned that you three would be living with Hector at the outskirts of this town," Duncan continued, "and he had his associates build that hideous fountain."

"Then he placed us inside," Isadora said, "and had us installed in the uptown courtyard, so he could keep an eye on us while he tried to hunt you down. We knew that you were our only chance of escaping."

The children reached a corner and stopped, while Duncan peeked around it to make sure no one was approaching. He signaled that it was safe, and continued the story. "We needed to send you a message, but we were afraid it would fall into the wrong hands. Isadora had the idea of writing in couplets, with our location hidden in the first letter of each line."

"And Duncan figured out how to get them to Hector's house," Isadora said. "He'd done some research about migration patterns in large black birds, so he knew that the crows would roost every night in Nevermore Tree—right next to Hector's house. Every morning, I would write a couplet, and the two of us would reach up through the fountain's beak."

"There was always a crow roosting on the very top of the fountain," Duncan said, "so we would wrap the scrap of paper around its leg. The paper was all wet from the fountain, so it would stick easily."

*"And Duncan's research was absolutely right.
The paper dried off, and fell at night."*

Isadora recited.

"That was a risky plan," Violet said.

"No riskier than breaking out of jail, and putting your lives in danger to rescue us," Duncan said, and looked at the Baudelaires in gratitude. "You saved our lives—again."

"We wouldn't leave you behind," Klaus said. "We refused to entertain the notion."

Isadora smiled, and patted Klaus's hand. "Meanwhile," she said, "while we were trying to contact you, Olaf hatched a plan to steal your fortune—and get rid of an old enemy at the same time."

"You mean Jacques," Violet said. "When we saw him with the Council of Elders, he was trying to tell us something. Why does he have the same tattoo as Olaf? Who is he?"

"His full name," Duncan said, flipping through his notebook, "is Jacques Snicket."

"That sounds familiar," Violet said.

"I'm not surprised," Duncan said. "Jacques Snicket is the brother of a man who—"

"There they are!" a voice cried, and in an instant the children realized they had neglected to look in back of them, as well as in front of them and around each corner. About two blocks behind them was Mr. Lesko, leading a small group of torch-carrying citizens straight up the street. The day was getting later, and the torches left long, skinny shadows on the sidewalk as if the mob were being led by slithering black serpents, instead of a man in plaid pants. "There are the orphans!" Mr. Lesko cried triumphantly. "After them, citizens!"

"Who are those other two?" asked an Elder in the crowd.

"Who cares?" said Mrs. Morrow, and waved her torch. "They're probably more accomplices! Let's burn them at the stake, too!"

"Why not?" said another Elder. "We already have torches and kindling, and I don't have anything else to do right now."

Mr. Lesko stopped at a corner and called down a street the children couldn't see. "Hey, everyone!" he shouted. "They're over here!"

The five children had been staring at the group of citizens, too terrified to get moving again. Sunny was the first to recover. "Lililk!" she shouted, and began crawling down the street as fast as she could. She meant something like "Let's go! Don't look behind you! Let's just try to get to Hector and his self-sustaining hot air mobile home before the mob catches up with us and burns us at the stake!" but her companions didn't need any encouragement. Down the street they raced, paying no attention to the footsteps and shouts behind them, which seemed to be growing in number as more and more people heard the news that V.F.D.'s prisoners were escaping. The children ran down narrow alleys and wide main streets, across parks and bridges that were all covered in black feathers. Occasionally they had to retrace their steps, a phrase which here means "turn around and run the other way when they saw townspeople approaching," and often they had to duck into doorways or hide behind shrubbery while angry citizens ran by, as if the children were playing a game of hide-and-go-seek instead of running for their lives. The afternoon wore on, and the shadows on V.F.D.'s streets grew longer and longer, and still the sidewalks echoed with the sounds of the mob's cries and the windows of the buildings reflected the flames from the torches the townspeople were carrying. Finally, the five children reached the outskirts of town, and stared at the flat, bare landscape. The Baudelaires searched desperately for a sign of the handyman and his invention, but only the shapes of Hector's house, the barn, and Nevermore Tree were visible on the horizon.

"Where's Hector?" Isadora asked frantically.

"I don't know," Violet said. "He said he'd be at the barn, but I don't see him."

"Where can we go?" Duncan cried. "We can't hide anywhere around here. The citizens will spot us in a second."

"We're trapped," Klaus said, his voice hoarse with panic.

"Vireo!" Sunny cried, which meant "Let's run—or, in my case, crawl—as fast as we can!"

"We'll never run fast enough," Violet said, pointing behind them. "Look."

The youngsters turned around, and saw the entire Village of Fowl Devotees, marching together in a huge group. They had rounded the last corner and were now heading straight toward the five children, their footsteps as loud as a roll of thunder. But the youngsters did not feel as if it was thunder that was rolling toward them. As hundreds of fierce and angry citizens approached, it felt more like the rolling of an enormous root vegetable. It felt like a root vegetable that could crush all of the reptiles in Uncle Monty's collection in five seconds flat, or one that could soak up every drop of water of Lake Lachrymose in an instant. The approaching crowd felt like a root vegetable that made every tree in the Finite Forest look like a tiny twig, made the huge lasagna served at the Prufrock Preparatory School cafeteria look like a light snack, and made the skyscraper at 667 Dark Avenue look like a dollhouse made for midget children to play with, a root vegetable so tremendous in size that it would win every first-place ribbon in every starchy farm crop competition in every state and county fair in the entire world from now until the end of time. The march of the torch-wielding mob, eager to capture Violet and Klaus and Sunny and Duncan and Isadora and burn each one of them at the stake, felt like the largest potato the Baudelaire orphans and the Quagmire triplets had ever encountered.

The Baudelaires looked at the Quagmires, and the Quagmires looked at the Baudelaires, and then all five children looked at the mob. All the members of the Council of Elders were walking together, their crow-shaped hats bobbing in unison. Mrs. Morrow was leading a chant of "Burn the orphans! Burn the orphans!" which the Verhoogen family was taking up with spirit, and Mr. Lesko's eyes were shining as brightly as his torch. The only person missing from the mob was Detective Dupin, who the children would have expected to be leading the crowd. Instead, Officer Luciana walked in front,

scowling below the visor of her helmet as she led the way in her shiny black boots. In one white-gloved hand she was clutching something covered in a blanket, and with the other hand she was pointing at the terrified children.

"There they are!" Officer Luciana cried, pointing her white-gloved finger at the five terrified children. "They have nowhere else to go!"

"She's right!" Klaus cried. "There's no way to escape!"

"Machina!" Sunny shrieked.

"There's no sign of deus ex machina, Sunny," Violet said, her eyes filling with tears. "I don't think anything helpful will arrive unexpectedly."

"Machina!" Sunny insisted, and pointed at the sky. The children took their eyes off the approaching mob and looked up, and there was the greatest example of deus ex machina they had ever seen. Floating just over the children's heads was the superlative sight of the self-sustaining hot air mobile home. Although the invention had been quite marvelous to look at in Hector's studio, it was truly wondrous now that it was actually being put to use, and even the angry citizens of V.F.D. stopped chasing the children for a moment, just so they could stare at this amazing sight. The self-sustaining hot air mobile home was enormous, as if an entire cottage had somehow detached itself from its neighborhood and was wandering around the sky. The twelve baskets were all connected and floating together like a group of rafts, with all of the tubes, pipes, and wires twisted around them like a huge piece of knitting. Above the baskets were dozens of balloons in varying shades of green. Fully inflated, they looked like a floating crop of crisp, ripe apples glistening in the last light of the afternoon. The mechanical devices were working at full force, with flashing lights, spinning gears, ringing bells, dripping faucets, whirring pulleys, and a hundred other gadgets all going at once, but miraculously, the entire self-sustaining hot air mobile home was as silent as a cloud. As the invention sailed toward the ground, the only sound that could be heard was Hector's triumphant shout.

"Here I am!" the handyman called from the control basket. "And here it is, like a bolt from the blue! Violet, your improvements are working perfectly. Climb aboard, and we'll escape from this wretched place." He flicked a bright yellow switch, and a long ladder made of rope began to unfurl down to where the children were standing. "Because my invention is self-sustaining," he explained, "it isn't designed to come back down to the ground, so you'll have to climb up this ladder."

Duncan caught the end of the ladder and held it for Isadora to climb up. "I'm Duncan Quagmire," he said quickly, "and this is my sister, Isadora."

"Yes, the Baudelaires have told me all about you," Hector said. "I'm glad you're coming along. Like all mechanical devices, the self-sustaining hot air mobile home actually needs several people to keep it running."

"Aha!" cried Mr. Lesko, as Isadora hurriedly climbed the ladder with Duncan right behind her. The mob had stopped staring at the deus ex machina and was now marching once again toward the children. "I *knew* it was a mechanical device! All those buttons and gears can't fool me!"

"Why, Hector!" an Elder said. "Rule #67 clearly states that no citizen is allowed to build or use any mechanical devices."

"Burn him at the stake, too!" cried Mrs. Morrow. "Somebody get extra kindling!"

Hector took a deep breath, and then called down to the mob without a trace of skittishness in his voice. "Nobody's going to be burned at the stake," he said firmly, as Isadora reached the top of the ladder and joined Hector in the control basket. "Burning people at the stake is a repulsive thing to do!"

"What's repulsive is your behavior," an

Elder replied. "The children have murdered Count Olaf, and you have built a mechanical device. You have both broken very important rules!"

"I don't want to live in a place with so many rules," Hector replied in a quiet voice, "or a place with so many crows. I'm floating away from here, and I'm taking these five children with me. The Baudelaires and the Quagmires have had a horrible time since their parents died. The Village of Fowl Devotees ought to be taking care of them, instead of accusing them of things and chasing them through the streets."

"But who's going to do our chores?" an Elder asked. "The Snack Hut is still full of dirty dishes from our hot fudge sundaes."

"You should do your own chores," the handyman said, as he leaned over to lift Duncan aboard his invention, "or take turns doing them according to a fair schedule. The aphorism is 'It takes a village to raise a child,' not 'Three children should clean up after a village.' Baudelaires, climb aboard. Let's leave these terrible people behind us."

The Baudelaires smiled at one another, and began climbing up the rope ladder. Violet went first, her hands clutching the scratchy rope as tightly as she could, and Klaus and Sunny followed closely behind. Hector turned a knob, and the mobile home rose up higher just as the crowd reached the end of the ladder. "They're getting away!" another Elder called, her crow-shaped hat bobbing with frustration. She jumped up to try to grab the edge of the ladder, but Hector had maneuvered his invention too high for her to reach. "The rulebreakers are getting away! Officer Luciana, do something!"

"I'll do something, all right," Officer Luciana said with a snarl, and tossed away the blanket she had been holding. From halfway down the ladder, the three climbing Baudelaires looked down and saw a large, wicked-looking object in Luciana's hands, with a bright red trigger and four long, sharp hooks. "You're not the only one with a mechanical device!" she called up to Hector. "This is a harpoon gun that my boyfriend bought for me. It fires four hooked harpoons, which are long spears perfect for popping balloons."

"Oh no!" Hector said, looking down at the climbing children.

"Raise the self-sustaining hot air mobile home, Hector!" Violet called. "We'll keep climbing!"

"Our Chief of Police is using a mechanical device?" Mrs. Morrow asked in astonishment. "That means she's breaking Rule #67, too."

"Officers of the law are allowed to break rules," Luciana said, aiming the harpoon gun in Hector's direction. "Besides, this is an emergency. We need to get those murderers down from there." Members of the mob looked at one another in confusion, but Luciana merely gave them a lipsticked smile, and pressed the harpoon gun's trigger with a sharp *click!* followed by a *swoosh!* as one of the hooked harpoons flew out of the gun straight toward Hector's invention. The handyman managed to manuever the self-sustaining hot air mobile home so the harpoon did not hit a balloon, but it struck a metal tank on the side of one of the baskets, making a large hole.

"Drat!" Hector said, as a purplish liquid began to pour out of the hole. "That's my supply of cranberry juice! Baudelaires, hurry up! If she causes any serious damage, we're all doomed!"

"We're coming as fast as we can!" Klaus cried, but as Hector moved his invention even higher in the air, the rope ladder was shaking so much that the Baudelaires could not move very fast at all.

Click! Swoosh! Another harpoon flew through the air and landed in the sixth basket, sending a cloud of brown dust fluttering to the ground, followed by some thin metal tubes. "She hit our supply of whole wheat flour," Hector cried, "and our box of extra batteries!"

"I'll hit a balloon with this one!" Officer Luciana called. "Then you'll fall to the ground, where we can burn you at the stake!"

"Officer Luciana," said one of the Council of Elders in the crowd, "I don't think you should break the rules in order to capture people who have broken the rules. It doesn't make sense."

"Hear, hear!" called out a townsperson from the opposite side of the crowd. "Why don't you put down the harpoon gun, and we'll walk over to Town Hall and have a council meeting."

"It's not cool," called out a voice, "to have meetings!" There was a rumble, as if another large potato had arrived, and the crowd parted to reveal Detective Dupin, riding through the mob on a motorcycle painted turquoise to match his blazer. Below his sunglasses was a grin of triumph, and his bare chest swelled with pride.

"Detective Dupin is using a mechanical device too?" an Elder asked. "We can't burn everyone at the stake!"

"Dupin isn't a citizen," another member of the Council pointed out, "so he's not breaking Rule #67."

"But he's riding through a crowd of people," Mr. Lesko said, "and he's not wearing a helmet. He's not showing good judgment, that's for sure."

Detective Dupin ignored Mr. Lesko's lecture about motorcycle safety and pulled to a stop beside Officer Luciana. "It's cool to be late," he said, and snapped his fingers. "I was buying today's edition of *The Daily Punctilio*."

"You shouldn't be buying newspapers," said an Elder, shaking his crow hat in disapproval. "You should be catching criminals."

"Hear, hear!" said several voices in agreement, but the crowd was beginning to look uncertain. It is hard work to be fierce all afternoon, and as the situation grew more complicated, the citizens of V.F.D. seemed a bit less bloodthirsty. A few townspeople even lowered their torches, which had been heavy to hold up all this time.

But Detective Dupin ignored this change in V.F.D.'s mob psychology. "Leave me alone, you crow-hatted fool," he said to the Elder, and snapped his fingers. "It's cool to fire away, Officer Luciana."

"It certainly is," Luciana said, and looked up into the sky to aim the harpoon gun again. But the self-sustaining hot air mobile home was no longer alone in the sky. In all the commotion, no one had noticed that the afternoon was over, and the V.F.D. crows had left their downtown roost to fly in circles before migrating to Nevermore Tree to spend the night as usual. Now the crows were arriving, thousands and thousands of them, and in seconds the evening sky was covered in black, muttering birds. Officer Luciana could not see Hector and his invention. Hector could not see the Baudelaires. And the Baudelaires could not see anything. The rope ladder was right in the path of the migrating crows, and the three children were absolutely surrounded by the birds of V.F.D. The wings of the crows rustled against the children, and their feathers became tangled in the ladder, and all the three siblings could do was hang on for dear life.

"Baudelaires!" Hector called down. "Hang on for dear life! I'm going to fly even higher, over the crows!"

"No!" Sunny cried, which meant something like, "I'm not sure that's the wisest plan—we won't survive a fall from such a height!" but Hector couldn't hear her over another *click!* and *swoosh!* from Luciana's harpoon gun. The Baudelaires felt the rope ladder jerk sharply in their hands, and then twist dizzily in the crow-filled air. From up in the control basket, the Quagmire triplets looked down and caught a glimpse, through the migrating crows, of some very bad news.

"The harpoon hit the ladder!" Isadora called down to her friends in despair. "The rope is coming unraveled!"

It was true. As the crows began to settle in

at Nevermore Tree, the Baudelaires could see more clearly, and they stared up at the ladder in horror. The harpoon was sticking out of one of the ladder's thick ropes, which was slowly uncurling around the hook. It reminded Violet of a time when she was much younger, and had begged her mother to braid her hair so she could look like a famous inventor she had seen in a magazine. Despite her mother's best efforts, the braids had not held their shape, and had come unraveled almost as soon as she had tied their ends with ribbons. Violet's hair had slowly spun out of the braid, just as the strands of rope were spinning out of the ladder now.

"Climb faster!" Duncan screamed down. "Climb faster!"

"No," Violet said quietly, and then said it again so her siblings could hear. More and more crows were taking their places in the tree, and Klaus and Sunny could see Violet's grim face as she looked down at them in despair. "No." The eldest Baudelaire took another look at the unraveling rope and saw that they couldn't possibly climb up to the basket of Hector's self-sustaining hot air mobile home. It was just as impossible as her mother ever braiding her hair again. "We can't do it," she said. "If we keep trying to climb up, we'll fall to our deaths. We have to climb down."

"But—" Klaus said.

"No," Violet said, and one tear rolled down her cheek. "We won't make it, Klaus."

"Yoil!" Sunny said.

"No," Violet said again, and looked her siblings in the eye. The three Baudelaires shared a moment of frustration and despair that they could not follow their friends, and then, without another word, they began climbing down the unraveling ladder, through the murder of crows still migrating to Nevermore Tree. When the Baudelaires climbed down nine rungs, the rope unbraided completely and dropped the children onto the flat landscape, unhappy but unharmed.

"Hector, maneuver your invention back down!" Isadora called. Her voice sounded a bit faint from so far away. "Duncan and I can lean out of the basket and make a human ladder! There's still time to retrieve them!"

"I can't," Hector said sadly, gazing down at the Baudelaires, who were standing up and untangling themselves from the fallen ladder, as Detective Dupin began to stride toward them in his plastic shoes. "It's not designed to return to the ground."

"There must be a way!" Duncan cried, but the self-sustaining hot air mobile home only floated farther away.

"We could try to climb Nevermore Tree," Klaus said, "and jump into the control basket from its highest branches."

Violet shook her head. "The tree is already half covered in crows," she said, "and Hector's invention is flying too high." She looked up in the sky and cupped her hands to her mouth so her voice could travel all the way up to her friends. "We can't reach you now!" she cried. "We'll try to catch up with you later!"

Isadora's voice came back so faintly that the Baudelaires could scarcely hear it over the muttering of the crows, who were still settling themselves in Nevermore Tree. "How can you catch up with us later," she called, "in the middle of the air?"

"I don't know!" Violet admitted. "But we'll find a way, I promise you!"

"In the meantime," Duncan called back, "take these!" The Baudelaires could see the triplet holding his dark green notebook, and Isadora holding hers, over the side of the basket. "This is all the information we have about Count Olaf's evil plan, and the secret of V.F.D., and Jacques Snicket's murder!" His voice was as trembly as it was faint, and the three siblings knew their friend was crying. "It's the least we can do!" he called.

"Take our notebooks, Baudelaires!" Isadora called, "and maybe someday we'll meet again!"

The Quagmire triplets dropped their note-books out of the self-sustaining hot air mobile home, and called out "Good-bye!" to the Bau-delaires, but their farewell was drowned out by the sound of another *click!* and another *swoosh!* as Officer Luciana fired one last harpoon. After so much practice, I'm sorry to say, her aim had improved, and the hook hit exactly what Luciana hoped it would. The sharp spear sailed through the air and hit not one but both Quagmire notebooks. There was a loud ripping noise, and then the air was filled with sheets of paper, tossing this way and that in the rustling wind made by the flying crows. The Quagmires yelled in frustration, and called one last thing down to their friends, but Hector's invention had flown too high for the Baudelaires to hear it all. ". . . volunteer . . ." the children heard dimly, and then the self-sustaining hot air bal-loon floated too high for the orphans to hear anything more.

"Tesper!" Sunny cried, which meant "Let's

try to gather up as many pages of the notebooks as we can!"

"If 'Tesper' means 'All is lost,' then that baby isn't so stupid after all," said Detective Dupin, who had reached the Baudelaires. He opened his blazer, exposing more of his pale and hairy chest, and took a rolled-up newspaper out of an inside pocket, looking down at the children as if they were three bugs he was about to squash. "I thought you'd want to see *The Daily Punctilio*," he said, and unrolled the newspaper to show them the headline. "BAUDELAIRE ORPHANS AT LARGE!" it read, using a phrase which here means "not in jail." Below the headline were three drawings, one of each sibling's face.

Detective Dupin removed his sunglasses so he could read the newspaper in the fading light. "Authorities are trying to capture Veronica, Klyde, and Susie Baudelaire," he read out loud, "who escaped from the uptown jail of the Village of Fowl Devotees, where they were

imprisoned for the murder of Count Omar."
He gave the children a nasty smile and threw
The Daily Punctilio down on the ground. "Some
names are wrong, of course," he said, "but every-
body makes mistakes. Tomorrow, of course,
there will be another special edition, and I'll
make sure that *The Daily Punctilio* gets every
detail correct in the story about Detective
Dupin's supercool capture of the notorious
Baudelaires."

Dupin leaned down to the children, so close
that they could smell the egg salad sandwich
he'd apparently eaten for lunch. "Of course,"
he said, in a quiet voice so only the siblings
could hear him, "one Baudelaire will escape
at the last minute, and live with me until
the fortune is mine. The question is, which
Baudelaire will that be? You still haven't let me
know your decision."

"We're not going to entertain that notion,
Olaf," Violet said bitterly.

"Oh no!" an Elder cried, and pointed out at

the flat horizon. By the light of the sunset, the Baudelaires could see a small, slender shape sticking out of the ground, while the Quagmire pages fluttered by. It was the last harpoon Luciana had fired, and it had hit something else after destroying the Quagmire notebooks. There, pinned to the ground, was one of the V.F.D. crows, opening its mouth in pain.

"You harmed a crow!" Mrs. Morrow said in horror, pointing at Officer Luciana. "That's Rule #1! That's the most important rule of all!"

"Oh, it's just a stupid bird," Detective Dupin said, turning to face the horrified citizens.

"A stupid bird?" an Elder repeated, his crow hat trembling in anger. "*A stupid bird?* Detective Dupin, this is the Village of Fowl Devotees, and—"

"Wait a minute!" interrupted a voice from the crowd. "Look, everyone! He has only one eyebrow!"

Detective Dupin, who had removed his sunglasses to read the paper, reached into the pocket of his blazer and put them back on again. "Lots of people have one eyebrow," he said, but the crowd paid no attention as mob psychology began to take hold again.

"Let's make him take off his shoes," Mr. Lesko called, and an Elder knelt down to grab one of Dupin's feet. "If he has a tattoo, let's burn him at the stake!"

"Hear, hear!" a group of citizens agreed.

"Now, wait just a minute!" Officer Luciana said, putting down the harpoon gun and looking at Dupin in concern.

"And let's burn Officer Luciana, too!" Mrs. Morrow said. "She wounded a crow!"

"We don't want all these torches to go to waste!" cried an Elder.

"Hear, hear!"

Detective Dupin opened his mouth to speak, and the children could see he was thinking frantically of something to say that would fool V.F.D.'s citizens. But then he simply closed his mouth, and with a flick of his foot, kicked the

Elder who was holding on to his shoe. As the mob gasped, the Elder's crow-shaped hat fell off as she rolled to the ground, still clutching Dupin's plastic shoe.

"It's the tattoo!" one of the Verhoogens cried, pointing at the eye on Detective Dupin's—or, more properly, Count Olaf's—left ankle. With a roar, Olaf ran back to his motorcycle and, with another roar, he started the engine. "Hop aboard, Esmé!" he called out to Officer Luciana. The Chief removed her motorcycle helmet with a smile, and the Baudelaires saw that it was indeed Esmé Squalor.

"It's Esmé Squalor!" an Elder cried. "She used to be the city's sixth most successful financial advisor, but now she works with Count Olaf!"

"I heard the two of them are dating!" Mrs. Morrow said in horror.

"We *are* dating!" Esmé cried in triumph. She climbed aboard Olaf's motorcycle and tossed her helmet to the ground, showing that she cared no more about motorcycle safety than she did about the welfare of crows.

"So long, Baudelaires!" Count Olaf called, zooming through the angry crowd. "I'll find you again, if the authorities don't find you first!"

Esmé cackled as the motorcycle roared off across the flat landscape at more than twice the legal speed limit, so within moments the motorcycle was as tiny a speck on the horizon as the self-sustaining hot air mobile home was in the sky. The mob stared after the two villains in disappointment.

"We'll never catch up to them," an Elder said with a frown. "Not without any mechanical devices."

"Never mind about that," another Elder replied. "We have more important things to attend to. Hurry, everyone! Rush this crow to the V.F.D. vet!"

The Baudelaires looked at one another in astonishment as the citizens of V.F.D. carefully unpinned the crow and began to carry it back into town. "What should we do?" Violet asked. She was talking to her siblings, but a member of the Council of Elders overheard and turned back to answer her. "Stay right here," he said. "Count Olaf and that dishonest girlfriend of his may have escaped, but you three are still criminals. We'll burn you at the stake as soon as this crow has received proper medical attention."

The Elder ran after the crow-carrying mob, and in a few seconds the children were alone on the flat landscape with only the shuffling papers of the Quagmire notebooks for company. "Let's gather these up," Klaus said, stooping down to pick up one badly ripped page. "They're our only hope of discovering the secret of V.F.D."

"And of defeating Count Olaf," Violet agreed, walking over to where a small stack of pages had blown together.

"Phelon!" Sunny said, scrambling after one that seemed to have a map scrawled on it. She meant "And of proving that we're not murderers!" and the children paused to look at *The*

Daily Punctilio, which still lay on the ground. Their own faces stared back at them, below the headline "BAUDELAIRE ORPHANS AT LARGE!" but the children did not feel at large. The Baudelaires felt as small as could be, standing alone on the bare outskirts of V.F.D., chasing down the few pages of the Quagmire notebooks that were not gone forever. Violet managed to grab six pages, and Klaus managed to grab seven, and Sunny managed to grab nine, but many of the recovered pages were ripped, or blank, or all crumpled from the wind.

"We'll study them later," Violet said, gathering the pages together and tying them in a bundle with her hair ribbon. "In the meantime, we have to get out of here before the mob returns."

"But where will we go?" Klaus asked.

"Burb," Sunny said, which meant "Anywhere, as long as it's out of town."

"Who will take care of us out there?" Klaus said, looking out on the flat horizon.

"Nobody," Violet said. "We'll have to take care of ourselves. We'll have to be self-sustaining."

"Like the hot air mobile home," Klaus said, "that could travel and survive all by itself."

"Like me," Sunny said, and abruptly stood up. Violet and Klaus gasped in surprise as their baby sister took her first wobbly steps, and then walked closely beside her, ready to catch her if she fell.

But she didn't fall. Sunny took a few more self-sustaining steps, and then the three Baudelaires stood together, casting long shadows across the horizon in the dying light of the sunset. They looked up to see a tiny dot in the sky, far far away, where the Quagmire triplets would live in safety with Hector. They looked out at the landscape, where Count Olaf had ridden off with Esmé Squalor, to find his associates and cook up another scheme. They looked back at Nevermore Tree, where the V.F.D. crows were muttering together for their evening roost, and then they looked out at the world, where families everywhere would soon be reading all about the three siblings in the special edition of *The Daily Punctilio*. It seemed to the Baudelaires that every creature in the world was being taken care of by others—every creature except for themselves.

But the children, of course, could care for one another, as they had been caring for one another since that terrible day at the beach. Violet, Klaus, and Sunny looked at one another and took a deep breath, gathering up all their courage to face all the bolts from the blue that they guessed—and, I'm sorry to say, guessed correctly—lay ahead of them, and then the self-sustaining Baudelaire orphans took their first steps away from town and toward the last few rays of the setting sun.

© Meredith Heuer

LEMONY SNICKET is the author of quite a few books, all dreadful, and has been accused of many crimes, all falsely. Until recently, he was living someplace else.

Visit him on the Web at www.lemonysnicket.com

BRETT HELQUIST was born in Ganado, Arizona, grew up in Orem, Utah, and now lives in New York City. He earned a bachelor's degree in fine arts from Brigham Young University and has been illustrating ever since. His art has appeared in many publications, including *Cricket* magazine and *The New York Times*.

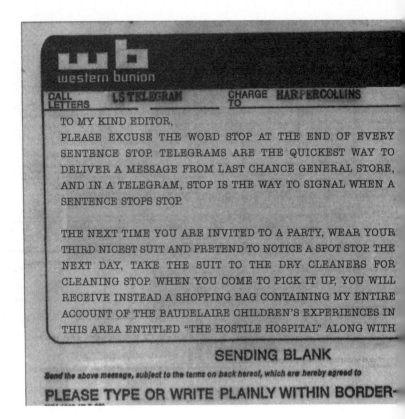

TO MY KIND EDITOR,

PLEASE EXCUSE THE WORD STOP AT THE END OF EVERY SENTENCE STOP. TELEGRAMS ARE THE QUICKEST WAY TO DELIVER A MESSAGE FROM LAST CHANCE GENERAL STORE, AND IN A TELEGRAM, STOP IS THE WAY TO SIGNAL WHEN A SENTENCE STOPS STOP.

THE NEXT TIME YOU ARE INVITED TO A PARTY, WEAR YOUR THIRD NICEST SUIT AND PRETEND TO NOTICE A SPOT STOP. THE NEXT DAY, TAKE THE SUIT TO THE DRY CLEANERS FOR CLEANING STOP. WHEN YOU COME TO PICK IT UP, YOU WILL RECEIVE INSTEAD A SHOPPING BAG CONTAINING MY ENTIRE ACCOUNT OF THE BAUDELAIRE CHILDREN'S EXPERIENCES IN THIS AREA ENTITLED "THE HOSTILE HOSPITAL" ALONG WITH

SENDING BLANK

AN INTERCOM SPEAKER, ONE OF THE LAMPS MISTAKENLY
DELIVERED TO HAL, AND A HEART-SHAPED BALLOON THAT HAS
POPPED STOP. I WILL ALSO INCLUDE A SKETCH OF THE KEY
TO THE LIBRARY OF RECORDS, SO THAT MR. HELQUIST CAN
ILLUSTRATE IT PROPERLY STOP.

REMEMBER, YOU ARE MY LAST HOPE THAT THE TALES OF THE
BAUDELAIRE ORPHANS CAN FINALLY BE TOLD TO THE GENERAL
PUBLIC STOP.

WITH ALL DUE RESPECT,
LEMONY SNICKET
PS YOUR SUIT WILL BE MAILED TO YOU LATER STOP.

.D

31901063655734